GERRY GOES TO SCHOOL

GERRY GOES TO SCHOOL

BY

ELINOR M. BRENT-DYER

W. & R. CHAMBERS, LTD.
LONDON AND EDINBURGH

Latest Reprint, 1952

Printed in Great Britain
by T. and A. CONSTABLE LTD., Hopetoun Street,
Printers to the University of Edinburgh

DEDICATED TO
HAZEL MARY BAINBRIDGE
WITH HEAPS OF LOVE FROM
' LEN '

CONTENTS.

GERRY GOES TO SCHOOL.

CHAPTER I.

AN INTERESTING LETTER.

THE Rev. Arthur Trevennor was reading his letters at breakfast, when he suddenly uttered a loud exclamation. His entire family stopped eating and looked at him in surprise.

'Anything up, pater?' asked his eldest son.

'Great-aunt Elinor is all right?' queried his wife anxiously. 'Oh, Arthur, I do hope nothing is the matter at Courdle Rigg!'

'Nothing is the matter at all,' he replied. 'At least—— Great Scott! How unusual!'

'What is unusual?' Margaret inquired, pausing in her task of spreading butter on Elizabeth's bread. 'Don't be aggravating, dear, but tell us straight out.'

Her father beamed at her as he replied, 'Sorry, Margot! Didn't know I was aggravating as a rule.—A most extraordinary thing indeed!' he went on, turning to his wife. 'I have just had a letter from Charlotte Challoner.'

'From Charlotte! Whatever has she to write about?' queried Mrs Trevennor with interest. 'It must be—let me see—it's at least ten years since you heard from them. Don't you remember, Arthur? They wrote to tell us about that little orphaned great-niece they were adopting. I don't think we have heard since, have we?'

'Who are the Challoners?' asked Helen at this point. 'I don't remember them, mummie.'

'No, dear; you wouldn't. They are old family friends.—Why have they written, dear?'

'Well, funnily enough, it's about that child,' replied her husband. 'Let me see—ah, here we are.

'"Doubtless you remember my telling you about the terrible accident, or, rather, infliction of God—for I can call a tornado nothing less —which brought about the death of our dear nephew, Gerald, and his wife. You will remember that I told you that we had decided to adopt their little daughter, Geraldine. We have had her for ten years now, and she is a dear child, and a great comfort to us. Unfortunately, now that dear Alicia has to go to Madeira she is rather an encumbrance. We do not wish to take her from England at her tender age—she is not yet twelve—and yet we are singularly destitute of relatives to whom we could commend her for the eighteen months we are likely to be absent. In our extremity I thought of you and your dear wife. Would you be so kind as to undertake the charge of Geraldine?

' "I know it is a very big thing to ask, but——" Um-um!' concluded the vicar, hurriedly folding up the letter with its old-fashioned Italian handwriting. 'That's all that matters.'

There was a momentary silence. Then Cecil broke it. 'Another girl!' he said disgustedly. 'What rot!'

'Nothing of the kind!' retorted Gillian, firing up at this insult to her sex. 'It's a jolly sight better than another boy, anyhow!'

'Gillian! You must not use such slang, dear!' protested her mother.

'It's ten-past eight,' interjected Paul. 'If you kids are going to catch the eight-seventeen, you'll have to make tracks!'

He rose himself as he spoke and made for the door, followed by the others. There was a hurried scramble in the old-fashioned hall, where Helen, Gillian, Lawrence, Cecil, Sheila, and Bernard wriggled into coats and caps, and collected school-bags. Margaret, six months emancipated from school, followed to help, and to see that Cecil, who suffered from a delicate chest, and was not to be trusted in such matters, wrapped himself up properly. Mrs Trevennor gave Paul his music and violin-case; and Elizabeth sent a plaintive wail after her elders of, 'Do bring me some post-cards to-day!'

When they were all gone the rector and his wife went back to the old-fashioned break-fast-room, where they took up their meal at the point at which they had left off. Margaret followed them; but Elizabeth, who had finished her bread-and-butter, slipped away to feed her rabbits.

Mrs Trevennor turned an anxious gaze on her husband. 'Arthur,' she said, 'we'll take her, of course?'

'Of course,' he replied. 'Where will you put her?'

His wife frowned as she thought matters over. 'Eleven years old,' she said slowly. 'That's too old to go with Betts and Sheila, and Helen and Gillian won't want any one else in their room.'

'Can't she share with Peggy?' inquired the rector.

Mrs Trevennor shook her head emphatically. 'Good gracious me, no! It's only a tiny room, and I couldn't possibly put another bed in it, could I, Pegs?'

'I'm afraid not, mother,' replied Margaret. 'But there's the box-room over the study. Turn the trunks out on to the attic-landing; put the cot bed down—I'll white enamel it if you like—you'll have to get some rugs; and Paul can stain the floor.'

'A chair from the guest-room,' Mrs Trevennor took up the tale. 'And there's the old white-painted dressing-table and washstand. You could enamel that too, dear, couldn't you? The wicker rocking-chair from the nursery; a few pictures and ornaments; and we must have it colour-washed again—pale pink, I think; don't you? Yes, we could make it very pretty; and it has a nice fireplace, and a good window.'

'With a lovely view,' chimed in Margaret. 'You can have my "Cherub Choir" if you like. And we can take "The Age of Innocence" from the guest-room, and "Cherry Ripe" from the nursery.'

Her mother turned to the rector, who had been sitting patiently waiting till

G.S.   B

his womenfolk should have finished their duologue.

'I think we can do it,' she said cheerfully. 'When will she come, dear?'

'Letter doesn't say,' he grunted. 'I suppose she'll come in a week or two. But I wonder if you have any idea as to what she will be like? It's years since I saw the Challoners; but I remember, even when I was a boy, they were considered old-fashioned, and I don't suppose they have marched with the times since. She'll probably be horrified at Jill's slang and Nell's hockey; she won't know any boys; and—oh, well, it's more your province than mine. Settle it to suit yourself! I don't mind!' With which summary, washing his hands of the affair, he got up and left the room.

As soon as he had gone Margaret turned eagerly to her mother. 'Mummie! Who are the Challoners? I remember hearing you and dad talk of them occasionally, but I don't really know anything about them. They're some sort of relation, aren't they?'

'They are your grandfather's cousins,' replied Mrs Trevennor; 'and when your father was a boy, they were very good to him. They are a very quaint pair—very old-fashioned and precise—so I expect Geraldine will be very unlike you girls. I don't suppose she has ever heard a word of slang in her life. And as for hockey and lacrosse, I rather imagine her hair will rise when she sees them. I shall put her in your charge, Peggy, when she does come. And see that the boys don't tease her too much, and make Jill treat her nicely.'

'I'll see she calls me "Margaret,"' replied the young lady decidedly.

Mrs Trevennor smiled apologetically. 'I'm sorry, dear! But, you see, you've been "Peggy" for so long that I forget still.'

'I don't see why you christened me "Margaret" when you will call me "Peggy,"' replied her daughter somewhat resentfully. 'And the others, too! We all have pretty names, and they're all shortened except Cecil and Paul!'

'Never mind that now! I'll try to remember, dear, but it's very difficult. Come upstairs with me and let us see what else we can think of to make Geraldine's room pretty. I want her to feel at home with us, poor baby! You'll have to help me, darling!' And Mrs Trevennor slipped a slender hand into her tall young daughter's arm, and looked up fondly into the lovely face.

Margaret relaxed in a moment. 'Come along, then, mother! We'll see what we can do for her! All the same,' she added laughingly, 'I'll bet any sum you like that she's "Gerry" and not "Geraldine" before she's been many hours here!'

CHAPTER II.

GERALDINE.

WHILE Margaret Trevennor and her mother were busily making a list of all that would be needed to set the box-room to rights, a small person, some three hundred and fifty miles away, was soberly trying to build a new world for herself from the fragments of the one which had, that morning, been shattered by Aunt Charlotte's statement.

'And now, Geraldine, my dear, I think it only right to tell you that we shall be unable to take you with us to Madeira. We have, therefore, written to an old friend, the Rector of Mordown, and have requested him to receive you into his family during the eighteen months your aunt Alicia and I shall be absent from England. I do not yet know whether he will accept the charge, but I consider it very probable that he will do so. I trust that, while you are at the Rectory, you will endeavour to be a credit to our training and care of you. Now you may go. It is nine o'clock, and you ought to be at the piano.'

'Yes, Aunt Charlotte.'

And Geraldine went meekly to the schoolroom, and sat down to practise scales and exercises with her fingers. Her mind was far enough away from her work. 'I wish,' she thought to herself—'I do wish that Aunt Charlotte and Aunt Alicia would send me to school; I don't want to go to a rectory! I want to go somewhere where there are ever so many girls who will play with me; I am so tired of being only one!'

At this point she went off into one of her 'imaginings,' in which she was at a large boarding-school, where everything went splendidly, and there were dozens and dozens of girls, who all wanted to play with her, and talk to her, and who called her 'Gerry.'

When she had got thus far Geraldine stopped abruptly in the middle of B major, and realised guiltily that she had spent an hour over six scales. She still had exercises, studies, and pieces to practise, and if she were to get through them all, she would have to begin at once. But how hard it was to keep one's thoughts on Czerny's *Études de la Velocité*! And even Beethoven, the beloved, seemed musicless this morning. For once in a way she was glad when eleven o'clock chimed from the clock on the mantelpiece, and she was free to drink the milk which Susie, the schoolroom maid, had brought half-an-hour previously.

If bonny Margaret had been able to peep in at the schoolroom window then, she would certainly have thought herself transported back to the times of the 'fifties.

The room was a sombre one, not in any way lightened by the green paper on the walls. An old-fashioned globe occupied one corner, and a strange instrument — a backboard — reigned over the other. Three or four steel engravings of religious pictures, a particularly ugly vase, and a bust of Shakespeare formed the decorations.

The quaintest part of the entire room, however, was Geraldine herself. She wore a gray dress, cut well off her shoulders, with a full skirt coming below the knees; her stockings were white, and her ankle-strap slippers were black. The long, brown hair, which had she been at the Rectory would have been plaited, was parted down the centre, and arranged in the tight corkscrew ringlets which one can see in portraits of the Princess Royal and Princess Alice as children. For the rest,

the curls framed a small, pale face with pointed
chin and short, straight nose. But I think
Margaret would have forgotten everything
else when she met Geraldine's eyes. They
were exceptionally lovely eyes, soft and
velvety-brown, with long black lashes, and
finely marked black brows. But Margaret
was not there; and after finishing her milk
Geraldine closed the piano, put her music
away, and walked sedately to the morning-
room, where her aunts and her needlework
awaited her, for, nominally, this was holiday-
time.

Helen and Gillian would almost have
fainted with horror had they been requested
to sit upright on a small stool stitching diligently at a strip of embroidery destined for
their own petticoats, and being 'seen, but not
heard.' Geraldine, however, was accustomed
to it, and she worked quietly until twelve,
when she got up, folded up her work and put
it away, and went to get herself ready for her
morning walk; not the jolly scamper and
scramble which the Rectory children meant
when they talked of 'going for a walk,' but
a sedate plodding along by the side of Aunt
Charlotte, with hands neatly gloved, and
carrying an umbrella. One might not even
speak unless spoken to; and Aunt Charlotte,

although genuinely fond of her little great-niece, did not appreciate the fact that when one is eleven one is not deeply interested in such questions as the boiling of puddings, or the making of flannel petticoats for the poor.

If Geraldine had been able to do as she liked, she would have danced along, asking eager questions about the Rectory at Mordown and its occupants. As it was, she stepped daintily along, answering her aunt's remarks with a demure, 'Yes, Aunt Charlotte'; 'No, Aunt Charlotte,' as conversation might demand.

After the walk, luncheon for the elders and dinner for Geraldine; and then she was expected to sit and sew till tea-time. After tea, from five till seven, was her free time, and she sat in the drawing-room reading her book till seven o'clock brought Susie and bed-time.

Three weeks later she was seated in the train by the side of Miller, the housemaid, on her way to Mordown. Aunt Charlotte had intended taking her; but Aunt Alicia had had what Miller described as a 'bad turn,' and could not be left. It was a long journey; and when they arrived at Mordown it was half-past eight, and Geraldine was sound asleep. Miller was preparing to shake her awake, when Paul Trevennor peered into the carriage.

'Asleep, is she?' he said to Miller. 'All right; don't wake her. I'll carry her out to the trap, if you'll cart her belongings out. I daren't wait; I've left Peggy with the reins, and Firefly is beastly fresh to-night.'

Not even the drive through the fresh, sharp air, cuddled up in Margaret's arms, awakened her. And when the rector came out to welcome the new-comer, he took a sleeping child out of his girl's arms, and carried her tenderly to the house, never waiting to hear Miller's explanation of her mistress's absence.

Indoors, Mrs Trevennor, helped by Margaret, took Geraldine upstairs to the pretty bedroom, undressed her, put her into one of Gillian's night-dresses, as her own were not unpacked, and tucked her into bed, all without once awaking her.

'Poor little dear!' said the rector's wife, as she pulled the bedclothes more cosily round her new charge; 'she must be simply worn-out. And her lashes are quite wet, Peggy. I hope she isn't afraid of us!'

'She'll be all right in the morning, mother,'

murmured Margaret. 'There! She's all right now; and when I come up I'll leave my door open; and if she wants anything in the night, I'll be certain to hear her, and I'll go to her at once.'

Geraldine slept all through the night and well on into the morning. Indeed, Miller, who had to return that day, had been gone two hours and more before she stirred.

When at length she woke up, she lay still for a few minutes, gazing at the pink walls and pretty arrangements, trying to 'tidy her mind,' as she later expressed it.

'Why, I've come to the Rectory,' she thought to herself. 'I wonder if it is late. But it must be, for the sun is quite bright. What a noise there is!'

And well might she think that; for it was Saturday, and the entire family was at home. And eleven o'clock on a Saturday morning at Mordown Rectory was not likely to be a quiet time. Presently she was aware of the door-handle turning, and then the door opened very quietly, and into the room came the loveliest girl Geraldine thought she had ever seen. She came up to the bed with a smile, and, bending down, kissed the little girl.

'Good-morning, Geraldine,' she said. 'I'm Margaret!'

Geraldine sat up, her eyes very bright, her cheeks flushed with pink. 'Oh!' she said with a gasp, 'are you real? Or are you a fairy princess?'

CHAPTER III.

TO say that Margaret Trevennor was startled is to put it very mildly. She would have been other than human had she not known that Heaven had gifted her with good looks. But never, during the whole of the nineteen years she had lived on earth, had she met with such whole-hearted admiration as the little stranger flung to her with such generous hands. As the eldest girl in a family of ten, she had been made to submit to candid criticism of a kind which left her with no illusions with regard to herself; therefore she had no idea of the burning adoration which welled up into Geraldine's heart at the sight of her dark eyes and hair, thrown up, as they were, by her delicately lovely colouring.

'You funny kid,' she said. 'Of course I'm real! You'll find that out jolly soon! Wherever is Nell? She's supposed to be bringing your breakfast up.—Nell!'

There was a rattling of china, accompanied

by the sound of careful footsteps, and in at the door came a tall, slender girl, as fair as Margaret was dark. She carried a daintily arranged tray, which she set down on the table by the bedside with a plump. Then she, too, came and kissed the little girl; but she did it in a carelessly off-hand way, unlike Margaret's. 'Hello!' she said. 'I'm Helen! 'How are you?'

'I thank you, I am very well,' replied Geraldine shyly.

Helen raised her eyebrows, and gave vent to a low whistle. 'I say, do you always talk like that?' she queried.

'I do not understand,' faltered Geraldine.

'Nell! Don't be horrid!' exclaimed Margaret, generously rushing to the rescue.— 'Come on, Geraldine! Try this mush! Topping with G.S. and milk.' And she ladled a goodly amount of golden syrup and milk over the porridge before she gave it to the small visitor.

'Be quick and mop it up!' urged Helen. 'It's a ripping morning, and we want to go down to the village to shop. Shall I take the top off your egg while you eat the mush?— Pegs, get her things ready!'

And as Margaret got up in obedience to perform this office, Geraldine noticed, for

the first time, how different were the clothes
these two girls wore from anything she had
been accustomed to see. The grounds of her
great-aunt's house were very wide; and,
except on Sunday, when she went to church
with them, she had never seen any girls of
her own age. And Dumberley had been
strangely deficient in little girls of her class,
so that, for the most part, the children she
saw were those from the cottages and the
farms round about. Now she noted that both
Margaret and Helen wore fresh white blouses,
with neatly knotted blue ties and blue skirts.
Margaret's came midway between her ankles
and her knees; but Helen's barely reached
her knees. The latter's long golden mane
was plaited back in one thick plait, and
finished off with a big black bow, and both
girls wore their hair parted at the side, just
like a boy. She just had time to notice this,
and then she saw that the clothes which
Margaret was taking from the wardrobe cup-
board were not those which she ordinarily
wore. She never learnt till years afterwards
that when Mrs Trevennor unpacked her box
she nearly cried over the old-fashioned frocks,
and straightway took a skirt which Gillian
had long outgrown, turned up the hem, and
took it in at the waist, and tucked petti-

coats, and sought out a white delaine blouse, and impounded a blue silk tie from Margaret, determined that at least the child should start fair where the boys were concerned. She knew that if once they saw her in that queer, old-fashioned dress they would torment her about it always.

So that when, finally, Geraldine was dressed, she looked just like any normal schoolgirl of twelve. Her hair was a difficulty, for she had no hair-ribbons, and Helen invariably possessed one only, and that the one she was wearing.

'Jill hasn't any either,' said Margaret in worried tones. 'Since we had her hair bobbed, she's just had a slide. Nell, are you sure you haven't any more?'

'Certain,' replied Helen.

'But, goodness! I gave you all mine when I put my hair up,' said her sister, touching somewhat self-consciously the glossy coils which were still not very well accustomed to their new arrangement. 'You can't have used all these in five months!'

'Have, then! This is the last! Betts got the pink for that party; and I made a pin-cushion cover out of the pale blue. Don't know where the brown is; and the other blacks got lost at odd times!'

Geraldine stood by, listening to this colloquy. She was too shy to suggest that her hair should be brushed over some one's finger into its usual ringlets. Besides, she had an idea that ringlets wouldn't look quite right with a blouse and skirt. Suddenly Helen gave an exclamation, 'Eureka! Got it! Just the thing! Hang on a jiff and I'll fetch it! Sha'n't be two wags of a dog's tail!' And with this, which was all so much Greek to the guest, she raced out of the room, presently returning with a length of broad scarlet ribbon, which she waved triumphantly. 'Just remembered my tennis bow! I sha'n't need it again for a while, and I can get some new then! Lucky I remembered it, isn't it? Will you plait her hair, or just tie it back?'

'Tie it back, I think,' said Margaret, as, with a comb, she tried to make a parting.—'Saint Anne! What heaps of hair you have, child! There, that's better!—Give me that slide from the table, Nell; I'm going to catch the sides up! Now, the other! There! Now for the ribbon!'

Geraldine stood quite still while this was going on. The two big girls twisted and turned her about as if she were a doll; but at length her toilet was finished, and Margaret

bade her look at herself in the glass. With
bated breath she did so.

It was a strange Geraldine whom she
saw reflected there. 'Why—why, I'm not
Geraldine at all now!' she said.

'No; you're Gerry,' replied Helen. 'Now,
come on downstairs, young un, and see if we
can find mother. Never mind your bed to-
day; Pegs will do it.' And with this she
pulled Geraldine, newly christened Gerry, out
of the room, and downstairs into a big, untidy
room, where a lady with fair hair and dark
eyes like Margaret's was sitting darning socks,
while at her feet cuddled a small, fair girl and
a boy who was possessed of the most cheerful
ugliness imaginable. At the table in the
middle of the room sat a fair-haired boy of
eleven or twelve, so like Helen that Geraldine
knew at once that he was a brother. Sprawled
on the sofa, reading a book, was another boy,
obviously another brother, since he was very
like Margaret. But the tall, black-haired
boy at the piano was so unlike the others that
the little girl wondered how he came to be
there.

Paul, for his part, saw only another school-
girl, clad in the regulation white and navy
blue which his own sisters wore. It did not
trouble him much. The child was too young

to interfere with him; and, in any case, she would be at school most of the week. He hoped she didn't strum. Sheila's five-finger exercises and stumblingly played scales were sufficiently irritating. Mrs Trevennor often said with a half-sigh that, with the exception of Helen, whose voice was in much demand at concerts and musical evenings, her own and her husband's musical gifts seemed to have passed the girls by. It is true Margaret could manage to accompany a simple song or strum a waltz, but Gillian's music-lessons had long since had to be given up, and Sheila was finding the path of music a hard one to follow. But Paul, Laurence, Bernard, and Cecil all played various instruments, and played them well. Laurence possessed a double-bass, Bernard a cello, and Cecil a viola. It was Paul, however, who was the star of the family; he was a brilliant pianist, and played the organ sufficiently well to be able to take the church services when need arose. But it was the violin on which he excelled. In his long, slender hands the instrument became a living creature, a will-o'-the-wisp of fancy; and even Gillian, the unmusical, had been known to weep when Paul played certain things.

Gerry did not know this at the time; she was to find it out later, but even then some subtle link seemed to bind her to the handsome lad with his dreamy gray eyes, who said nothing when she came in, but merely nodded a smiling greeting at her.   However, she had not much time for private thought, for Mrs Trevennor had risen from her chair with a fine disregard for her lapful of mending, and, crossing the floor hurriedly, took the little visitor into her arms and kissed her tenderly, as Gerry never remembered to have been kissed before.   'Welcome, darling!' she said.   'A thousand welcomes to you! I'm so glad you've come at last; we've all been looking forward to your coming, haven't we?' and she flashed a glance round the room.   Under the influence of that look the two middle boys got up and came forward to shake hands. 'This is Cecil,' said their mother, indicating the younger boy; 'and this is Laurence. These two small people are Sheila and Geoffrey,' she added, as with a dexterous wheeling movement she brought them into the circle.   Fair-haired Sheila came forward, lifting her face for the kiss which Gerry gave her rather shyly; but Geoffrey kept well back and stared at the visitor with wide brown eyes, which were his only claim to good looks.

'Will she stay always?' he demanded finally.

'We hope so, sonnie,' replied his mother. Then, knowing that her youngest son was best left to himself, she turned to her first-born with a pleading air. 'This is Paul, Gerry.'

Paul rose to his feet and came forward. 'Hello!' he said cheerfully. 'You look rather more alive than you did when I first saw you. You were sound asleep last night.'

'Was I?' said Gerry shyly.

'Yes; rather! Why, I carried you to the trap, and gave you to Peggy, and you never even stirred, never batted an eyelid.'

Gerry looked as she felt, alarmed. Paul, who for all his dreamy temperament was fond of teasing, laid a hand on her shoulder. 'I think you owe me something for carrying you,' he said laughingly.

His mother, who had been summoned to the window by the old gardener, did not notice him; and Helen had run out of the room to fetch Gillian, Bernard, and Elizabeth. In all justice to Paul, it must be said that he had no idea of the type of child which stood before him, or he would never have teased her.

Gerry, who had no experience of boys and their ways, took it all in deadly earnest. 'I— I am sorry,' she faltered. 'How much do I owe you?'

Paul looked at her laughingly. To him

she was just a little girl like Sheila. Gerry was small for her age, and very childish-looking, so he said good-naturedly, 'Oh, well, give me a kiss and we'll cry quits!'

Poor Gerry! Already, within the course of one hour, she had been kissed oftener than she usually was in a month. Geoffrey's wide eyes were still glued to her face; she felt strange in her short skirts and tied-back curls; and she had never kissed a single man in her life. So when Paul bent his fine face down to her she shrank back, exclaiming piteously, 'Oh no, no! I cannot! Please do not ask it!'

Paul stared.

His mother, attracted by the agony in the little girl's voice, turned round. 'Paul,' she cried, 'you are not to tease Gerry!—Never mind him, dear! It's only fun! What did he want you to do?' She crossed the room to Gerry's side as she spoke, and slipped a protecting arm round the little girl's shoulders.

'It's too bad of you, Paul!' she said indignantly. 'What were you doing to her?'

'I—I only asked her for a kiss,' mumbled Paul. 'I didn't know she'd be funky.—I sha'n't bite you, kid,' he added to the little guest.

Something in the half-shamed, half-laughing tones of his voice attracted Gerry. She lifted her great brown eyes to his face. What she saw there reassured her, and, holding out her slim little hand, she said, 'I—I did not know it was a joke. I beg your pardon. I will— k-kiss you if you like.' And with this she turned up to his her face, flushed with the effort she was making.

Paul bent once more and kissed her heartily. 'That's right,' he said. 'We'll be pals, shall we?'

'Oh yes,' replied Geraldine sweetly. She hadn't the remotest idea of what a 'pal' might be, but she felt that she could trust him.

'Come on, Gerry!' cried Helen's voice at this moment. 'Here's the rest of us—Jill, Bear, and Betty!'

Gerry turned round. Standing before her was a jolly, brown-eyed boy of fourteen; a small girl, also brown of eyes and hair; and a girl rather older than herself, whose little, dark face was hard and unfriendly. 'How do you do?' she said shyly to these new-comers.

'Hello!' said the boy. 'So you're Gerry?' Baby Elizabeth demanded a kiss as her right. But Jill, after a muttered 'Hello!' turned away, and busied herself with Cecil's stamps.

Gerry looked at her in dismay. This was the first unfriendliness she had met with, and it hurt her. The others took no notice of it. They were used to Jill's 'moods.' And when she refused to join the shopping-party, nobody troubled much; but Gerry felt that here was an enemy, and one who would not be easily placated.

CHAPTER IV.

'AUTRE TEMPS, AUTRE MŒURS.'

EVEN outdoor things were changed for Gerry. Her bonnet and old-fashioned pelisse had vanished as mysteriously as had her old dress. Instead, she found waiting for her a reefer-jacket and a scarlet tam like the ones Helen and Sheila wore. A pair of brown walking-shoes were produced, and then she was pronounced 'ready.'

'But I have no gloves,' she said timidly to Helen.

That young lady stared at her. 'What on earth d' you want with gloves?' she demanded. 'We aren't going to the town—only to the village—and it isn't cold! For goodness' sake don't let Jill hear you, or she'll rag the life out of you!'

This final hint sealed the question. For some reason or other Gerry felt that Jill was her determined enemy, and she would rather have stood teasing from the entire family than endure Jill's scorn. She was an impulsive little person, although her training up to the

present had taught her self-control, and she
had taken a great liking to the third Rectory
girl. Gillian's vivid, impish face, with its
determined mouth and quick-glancing eyes,
was unlike anything she had ever seen before.
In her own mind she compared Jill to 'Airy
Fairy Lilian':

> From beneath her gathered wimple
> Glancing with black-beaded eyes.

'That might just have been written for her,'
she thought, unaware that the Rectory children
scorned the gentle poet of the Victorian era,
and would have shouted with derision could
they have read her thoughts.

'Well, wake up!' said Helen impatiently.
'For goodness' sake don't dream! One in the
family's quite enough, thank you!'

'Gerry, d'you like hockey?' asked Sheila
as they went down the path. 'I do! I'm in
the Sixth Eleven, and Nell says if I work I
might get into the Fifth. Nell's captain,
you see!'

'Jolly good game,' remarked Nell complacently. 'We miss Peggy, though! She
was a ripping wing! Where d'you play,
Gerry? Forward, I should think,' running
her eyes over the visitor's slight figure.
'D'you play left or right? Which?'

'Left or right what?' gasped Gerry, so

startled that she forgot all Great-aunt Charlotte's canons of good behaviour.

Nell's gray eyes opened widely. 'D'you mean to say you don't know hockey?' she said incredulously.

Margaret, who was a little in advance with Laurence and Bernard, caught the word 'hockey,' and, turning round, smiled infectiously at the guest. 'Oh, you'll soon know all about it!' she said.—'Nell, do haul Cecil out of that ditch! He'll be having another of his bad colds!—There! I knew Geoff would want to be carried!—Paul, you should let him walk! He can't be tired yet!—Get down, Geoff! You aren't a baby now!'

'S'a'n't,' said Geoff with cool audacity, clinging so tightly round Paul's neck as he spoke that he nearly strangled his brother; while, to Gerry's amazement, Helen made a dash after Cecil, who had been parading along the leaf-lined ditch, and hauled him forth on to the road with more vigour than decorum.

'Get on to the road, you little nuisance!' exclaimed his sister. 'You'll cough the house down to-morrow, I suppose!—D'you think he'd better go back home and change his shoes and stockings, Peg?'

'P'r'aps he'd better,' began Margaret doubtfully. But the culprit twisted himself out
of Helen's grasp, and settled the matter by
darting down the road at the top of his
speed. With a yell of 'Tally-ho!' Bernard
tore after him, and Margaret shrugged her
shoulders resignedly. 'It's useless trying to
boss him,' she explained to Gerry, who had
been a silent, though horrified, spectator of
this cool disregard for law and order. 'This
is the church, Gerry. Isn't it beautiful?
We haven't time to go in now, but some
of us will be coming to Evensong at six,
and you can come then. Mother's going
to take you into town this afternoon, to get
your school uniform, and so on. Didn't you
know?' she added, seeing incredulity in the
big eyes raised to hers. 'You're going to
school with the others—to St Peter's. We
can't run to a good governess plus finishing
master, so we've all attended St Peter's.
Nell is hockey captain there, and Jill is
captain of the Middle School. Bernard and
Cecil go to the boys' St Peter's, and Larry
was there till last year. Then he won a
scholarship to St John's—that's the big day
public school at Greylands, three stations
farther on. We're hoping Jill and he will go
to the 'Varsity. They're the brainy members

of the family. I'm a duffer, and Nell's best at games.'

'I'm going to be a gym. mistress,' chimed in Helen. 'Jill wants to be a doctor, but it all costs money; and we're a crush, you see.'

'Paul's going to be a musician,' added Sheila, who had been dancing along by Gerry's side in a way which would have filled Great-aunt Charlotte's heart with horror and consternation. 'Bear wants to go farming in Canada or Australia——'

'I'm going to be a sailor,' came from Paul's shoulder. 'What are you going to do, Gerry?'

'I don't know,' faltered Gerry, who felt that she had indeed got into a new world. Great-aunt Charlotte always spoke pityingly of Dr Sinclair's daughter, who came up to the Hall every day to give Gerry her lessons; and Great-aunt Alicia had shaken her head, and declared that she did not know what the world was coming to in these days, when young ladies left the shelter of their homes and went out to work. Yet here were the rector's daughters calmly talking of their future in terms of work, and, what was more, actually taking pride in Jill's ambition to be a doctor. But worse was yet to come.

'Cecil wants to be an actor,' went on Margaret calmly. 'He is certainly very clever that way, and if he only grows stronger, and still wishes it in a year or two, he will be sent to an acting school. Uncle Hervey is his godfather, and he's paying for his education, and he says that if that's what Ces wants, he shall have it!'

The Misses Challoner had always regarded the theatre and all its works as the depth of iniquity, and had imbued their little great-niece with the same views. Gerry stood stock-still in the middle of the road, regardless of etiquette and the training she had received, and cried, 'But it's wicked! Your papa can't want Cecil to go to a wicked place and become a bad man! And all actors are bad. Great-aunt Alicia said so.'

'Well! For the love of Mike!' gasped Laurence. Margaret looked pleadingly at him; while Paul, setting Geoff on the ground, said, 'Wicked? What awful rot! It's no more wicked than any other profession! It's what you like to make of it! It's just as easy for a clergyman to be wicked as it is for an actor! And just as easy for either to be straight and decent! Excuse me, Gerry, but what ghastly tosh your aunts seem to have talked!'

Gerry looked scandalised. The habits and ways of thinking of a lifetime are not easily broken, and she was very much Geraldine as she replied, 'I beg your pardon, but it is my great-aunts of whom you are speaking!'

Paul laughed as he replied easily, 'My dear kid, I know that! But it doesn't alter the fact that they talk tosh. Now, keep your hair on,' he added, as Gerry's eyes flashed and her cheek crimsoned with anger. 'I dare say they're very estimable ladies and so on, but they must know nothing about the stage or they wouldn't talk such blither.'

'Ra-ther not!' chimed in Laurence. 'Why, some of the noblest men alive to-day are actors, and don't you forget it!'

'Boys! Boys! Don't talk to Gerry like that,' interposed Margaret, her lovely face flushed with distress. 'She doesn't understand, that's all.—Gerry, they don't mean to be disrespectful to your great-aunts. Don't mind them, but come along in with me to see if Geoff's boots are finished.'

Whether Gerry would have consented to this suggestion or not will never be known, for at that moment Cecil and Bernard came racing back with some news which they both tried to tell at once. The running and the shouting together brought on Cecil's cough, Geoff yelled to be picked up again, and in the general pandemonium Gerry's outburst was forgotten. When, finally, things were quietened, Margaret, Paul, the two little ones, and Gerry decided to do the shopping at one side of the street, while the others went on to pay two visits on the other. In the shops Gerry stood demurely by while Margaret gave her orders; and Sheila and Geoff, shepherded by Paul, gazed into the windows. In the meantime, Helen, with her escort of three, strolled leisurely down the street.

'By George! What a spitfire!' observed Laurence, as soon as they were out of hearing. 'Didn't think she had it in her; did you, Nell?'

'Never thought about it at all,' replied Helen. 'Here we are at Mrs Brown's. Will you three wait while I go in? Or will you come with me?'

'What is it? New baby, or bad leg?' asked Laurence cautiously.

'New baby,' replied his sister.

'Then I'm not coming! They always expect you to hold the creatures, an' I'm terrified of dropping 'em! We'll wait here for you.'

'All right!—Good-morning, Gladys! I've

called to see your mother. How is she this morning?'

Gladys Brown, a stolid, round-faced girl of thirteen, afflicted with adenoids and a perpetual cold, held the door open silently, and Helen vanished into the room beyond, while the three brothers propped themselves up against the wall.

'Who's the spitfire?' queried Bernard.

'Gerry! Blazed up like a little fury because old Paul said something about her precious aunts she didn't approve of.'

'Like a girl!' observed Cecil. 'Rummiest creatures out!'

'Um! I say, there's going to be fireworks with Jill,' added Bernard. 'She simply hates Gerry.'

'What for?' demanded Laurence. 'I don't see how she can hate her. She hasn't seen her more 'n five minutes.'

Bernard laughed. 'Think I don't know Jilly by this time? It's war to the knife with her an' Gerry! An' I can't think why,' he added reflectively.

'I can,' replied Cecil. 'She's jealous because Paul likes Gerry! That's why.'

'Jealous! Jill! What rot you do talk!' laughed Bernard. 'Why on earth should she be jealous? Why, she's never even been specially fond of old Paul! You're talking through your hat, Ces!'

But Larry looked serious. He knew that, partly through his continued delicacy, partly as a natural gift, Cecil was far more observant than any of them. They all knew that Jill was a jealous little creature where Bernard, her beloved twin, was concerned, and it was quite possible that she might extend that jealousy over Paul, or, indeed, any of them. He could not remember whether Jill had been in the room when his eldest brother had made that compact of palship with the little new-comer. If she had been, the odds were that it was that which lay at the root of this present 'mood.'

'Was Jill in when Paul was teasing Gerry?' he suddenly demanded of his younger brother.

Cecil gave him a quick look as he replied, 'Only part of the time.'

'D'you mean when they were palling up?' asked Bernard. 'What rot! As though that would upset Jill!'

'All the same,' replied Laurence, 'I'll bet you what you like that's what's done it!— That's what you're driving at, isn't it, kid?' he added to Cecil.

The younger boy grinned at him. 'Think

you're precious clever, don't you, old Larry?'
he observed. 'Twigged on the moment.'

'Oh, well, what's it matter? Gerry can
look after herself,' replied Bernard.

But Laurence still looked disturbed. 'That's
just what I'm afraid she can't do,' he said.
'She's new to our ways; she's like no kid
I've ever met; and Jill can be a regular little
beast when she likes!'

'Here! That's enough about Jill!' retorted
Bernard, firing up in defence of his twin.
'You let Jill alone! See? If you want to
go knight-erranting, chase round after Gerry,
but Jill's my affair!'

'Then see and make her behave herself!'
returned Laurence. 'And don't give me any
more cheek, young man, or you'll be wishing
you wasn't you!'

Laurence's arm was strong, and Bernard
had no desire to be thrashed unnecessarily,
so, for the present, he cooled down.

Helen came out of the cottage just then,
and they all trotted down the road to the
next place of call, where they trooped in
to see Georgie Bartlett. Georgie was the
leading choir-boy. He was possessed of an
exquisite voice, an angelic face, and at least
three times his own share of mischief. This
last had led him to attempt to ride on the

back of a cart, from which he had fallen, breaking his collar-bone, spraining an ankle and a wrist, and generally bruising himself. He and Cecil had been great chums until the rector had been obliged to lay an embargo on the friendship; Georgie's mischief led Cecil into places where colds were easily caught, and after two bronchial attacks had followed two successive expeditions to the river, Cecil had been forbidden to go there or anywhere with Georgie unless one of the older boys was with them. Still, Georgie was a great favourite at the Rectory, and they all stayed talking to him till Mrs Bartlett turned them out with the grim remark that if Georgie didn't kill himself, they would do it for him, since his 'temperature would be the Lord knew where!'

By that time it was nearly one o'clock, and they had to race home in order to be in time for dinner. They found the others seated round the table; and Laurence frowned as he noticed that their mother had in all innocence placed Gerry next to Jill, who was looking like a thunder-cloud personified.

'Mark my words, there'll be squalls!' remarked Cecil, as they tore upstairs to the bathroom to wash their hands.

What more he might have said was prevented by the rector's calling upstairs, 'Cecil,

if you haven't changed your shoes and stockings, go and do so immediately!'

Cecil went; but as he left the room he
winked expressively at his elder brother, with
the remark, 'Get out the gamps!   Jill's looking for trouble!'

CHAPTER V.

'CECIL, have you got your scarf on?'
'Hang it all! Who's touched my
Pro Milone?'

'Merciful heavens! Here's my French
exercise at last! Well, that's a good thing!
Maddy would have been furious if I'd turned
up without it!'

'Jill dear, you'll look after Gerry, won't
you? Tell her where to go, and so on?
She won't be able to depend on Nell; and
Sheila is a broken reed, though she means
well.'

'Here you are, Gerry; here's your pass.
Put it into that little pocket inside your coat,
and don't lose it! Good-bye, my child!
Good luck!' And the rector bent to kiss
the child who had been entrusted to his care,
smiling into the big eyes which looked at him
so gravely.

It was Monday morning. Gerry had been
at the Rectory for two days now. Those two
days loomed large in her experience; all the

rest of her life seemed unreal and dream-like in comparison, and, like the market-woman in the nursery rhyme, she was beginning to wonder 'if this be I.' Saturday afternoon had been a skurry into the town with Mrs Trevennor, Helen, and Jill, where she had been provided with a short serge gym. tunic, three white blouses, a big navy blue coat, and little black velvet cap with the school crest stitched on it. That was for everyday. Then, for best, there had been a neat little navy blue costume, a couple of white silk shirt blouses, and a big black velours hat with a black band round it—just the same kind of hat as Helen and Jill and Sheila possessed; black shoes and stockings were provided for everyday wear, and there were brown ones to wear with the costume. Some hair-ribbons and a couple of ties were added, and then Mrs Trevennor decided that they had done enough for that day.

'You see, dear,' she explained to Gerry as they sat in the café afterwards eating delicious cream-cakes and drinking tea, 'your clothes are very nice, but your aunts thought you might need one or two things, and told me to get what you needed. We will have the blue frock altered a little—it will be rather chilly for the winter with that low neck and these short sleeves, and I think you will feel more comfy if the skirt is not quite so full. We'll alter the white muslins as well, and then you'll be all right. Have another cream-cake? Nell and Jill love them when we come here for tea as a treat.'

After tea Mrs Trevennor had taken Jill to the hairdresser's to have her hair cut; and Helen had walked Gerry round to the schools, where she pointed out various marks of interest. Then they had come home; and after supper Margaret had escorted Jill, Bernard, Gerry, Cecil, and Sheila to bed, where the little guest had fallen asleep as soon as her head touched the pillow.

Sunday had proved even more unusual at the Rectory than Saturday. To begin with, there had been no Collect or chapter to learn. After breakfast, which was at nine o'clock, every one had dispersed to fulfil certain duties, for the rector liked his maids to be free to attend the services. So Margaret went to the kitchen to help cook; Helen and Jill made the beds; the boys brought in wood and coal, and cleaned the boots; Sheila played with Geoff and Betty to keep them quiet; and Gerry was requested to help Mrs Trevennor as she dusted the study and tidied the books.

Then came the changing into her new costume, and standing still while Margaret plaited her hair into a long, thick plait, and tied it with the wide scarlet ribbon. The jolly walk to church, between Paul and Mrs Trevennor, was so unlike the prim walks with Great-aunt Charlotte, and the service was so bright and pleasant. The rector preached a ten-minutes' sermon, so simple that the smallest child could understand it, and yet so wise that the oldest could not fail to be interested.

After church came dinner; and then, while her mother rested, Margaret called the younger ones round her and read aloud to them. Helen and Paul had classes in the Sunday School, and set out with their father; Laurence and Bernard and Jill prepared their divinity for the next day's lesson. It was all so quiet, and yet so unlike the Dumberley Sundays. Then came tea and hymn-singing, and the older members of the family, down to Cecil, went to Evensong. When they came back supper was waiting; and then came bed, and sleep.

And now Monday had come, and, at long last, Gerry was going to school. She could scarcely stand still as Helen plaited her hair, and tied it with one of the new black ribbons.

She felt rather self-conscious in her gym. tunic, for it was even shorter than her costume skirt; but she observed that the others wore tunics just as short and no one noticed it, so she took comfort in the fact. Breakfast was the usual scramble of schooldays, and after it was consumed there was a rush for coats and caps—which brings us to the beginning of this chapter.

As her father kissed Gerry, Jill looked across with scorn in her dark eyes.

'Jill dear,' said her mother again, 'you will look after Gerry, won't you, and give her a helping hand?'

Jill wriggled impatiently from the gentle grasp. 'Oh yes,' she said indifferently. 'If she needs anything, I'll help her. But it's best to stand on one's own feet.' And with this she opened the front-door and walked out.

Mrs Trevennor sighed. Jill had always been the 'difficult' one of the family. She could always be relied on to be either angelic, or else so naughty that she was unbearable. No half-measures for Jill. She did every-thing thoroughly. At present she was being as perverse where Gerry was concerned as it was possible to be. Helen overheard the sigh. 'All right, mummie,' she said;

'I'll give an eye to Gerry. Don't worry.' And with that Mrs Trevennor had to be content.

Down the road they went, long-legged Helen swinging her fair plait as she walked; Sheila trotting along, her short curls bobbing gaily beneath her cap; Gerry clinging to Helen's side, her eyes wide with half-frightened, half-pleasurable anticipation. Behind them came the boys, wrangling amicably upon the chances of the Harlequins in a forthcoming match; and ahead of them all marched Jill, every line of her figure showing determination.

'I should like to give her a sound shaking,' thought Helen to herself. Then she turned to Gerry. 'It will be all right, Gerry, old thing. Not funking it, are you?'

Gerry was not sure of the meaning of the word 'funking,' but Helen's tone gave her her cue, and her 'Oh no!' was as firm as if she had understood.

'That's right,' said Helen in relieved tones. 'Never funk anything that you're up against. Simply go for it, and flatten it out!'

'Yes,' said Gerry meekly.

'I'm Senior House, of course, and you'll be Junior or Middle School, so we sha'n't see a fearful lot of each other. But stand the racket all you can, and if it gets beyond

you, come to me. You've only two things
to remember—play the game, and don't cry
when you're down.'

This brought them to the station, and with
a sigh of relief Helen turned away to catch
Jill.

'Jill, you're being a perfect little beast!
You hurt mummie horribly just now; and if
you aren't decent to that poor kid, I'll make
you pay for it,' she said decisively.

Jill lifted angry eyes to her sister's face.
'P'r'aps you'll kindly mind your own business and leave me to mind mine,' she said
furiously. 'You seem to think that 'cos
you're hockey captain you can do as you
like! It's about time you understood that
you can't! Out of the hockey-field I won't
be bossed by you, so stop it!' And with
that she stalked off, leaving Helen filled with
dismay.

'Leave her alone,' said Laurence's voice
behind her. 'I did think you had more tact,
Nell! There's nothing for it but leaving her
to herself when she's like that. As for Gerry,
the kid's got plenty of pluck, and she'll get on
all right, you'll see.'

Just then the train came in, and in the
hurry of getting all the junior members of the
family into the carriage Helen had no time to

reply to his strictures. In the carriage were two of her own particular chums, Madeleine Carew and Claire Ashe, and to them she introduced Gerry. The two big girls were kindly enough, but it was scarcely to be expected that they should take much interest in a small girl of twelve. Jill had forgathered with Claire's younger sister, Naïda ; and Sheila had slipped down the corridor into the next compartment, where Muriel Hatherley and Allegra Atherton were giggling together over a masterly sketch by Allegra of mademoiselle scolding Janie Ferrers. Helen soon became absorbed in hockey talk, most of which was Greek to Gerry ; and Jill turned a determined back on her, so the new-comer felt out of it. She would have given much at that moment to have been able to cry ; but pride kept back the tears, and she sat very upright watching the trees fly past. Suddenly a shadow fell across the compartment, and Jill's voice exclaimed joyfully, 'Rosamund Atherton! What luck! Come and sit down here and tell us about the concert!'

'Nothing much to tell,' replied Rosamund, sitting down nevertheless. 'I've got the programme at home. If you want to see it, I'll fetch it to-morrow ; but I thought you weren't keen on music, Jill?'

'I'm not awfully,' returned Jill truthfully; 'but Mavie Dunne is an O.G. of S.P.H.S., and, of course, I'm interested that way.'

'Well, it was awfully jolly, and Mavie plays beautifully. Mother says she ought to be great when she's grown a little older,' replied Rosamund, as she glanced across the carriage. 'Jill, who is that new girl over there? D'you know her?'

'Yes, worse luck! That's the freak that's living with us,' replied Jill.

She was careful to speak so that Helen did not hear her; but her words reached Gerry's preternaturally fine ears, and she coloured hotly.

'Jill!' cried Rosamund. 'She *heard* you!'

'Well, she shouldn't listen to private conversation, then,' returned Jill, nevertheless looking, as she felt, rather uncomfortable.

'I'm going to speak to her,' said Rosamund with determination, and leaving her seat, she went and sat down by Gerry.

'Hello! I'm Rosamund Atherton. Jill Trevennor says you are living with them, so I know you must be Geraldine Challoner,' she began. 'You're going to St Peter's. I think you'll like it. It's a ripping school.'

Helen glanced up, and a feeling of relief took possession of her. If Rosamund Atherton espoused Gerry's cause, the child would be all right.

Meanwhile Gerry, looking up shyly, saw a charming face smiling at her out of friendly blue eyes, and her heart grew suddenly lighter as she smiled back.

'I expect you'll have a ripping time,' pursued Rosamund. 'I wonder what form you'll be in! How old are you?'

'Twelve,' said Gerry.

'A year younger than I am,' returned Rosamund. 'I expect you'll be in the same form as my sister Con. Would you like to know her? She's a little farther down. Come along and see her.'

'I—if—if Nell says I may,' began Gerry.

'Oh, that's all right,' replied Rosamund. 'She'll know you're with me, and we can't interrupt *them*! They're fixing the team for Saturday.'

And without further ado she caught Gerry's hand, and tugged her out of the compartment and into another, where Sheila sat with four other girls, two of whom were chattering gaily to her, while the other two were reading. They all put down their books as the two entered, and Sheila smiled, and said, 'Hello, Gerry!'

'These are my sisters, Francesca, and Con,

and Allegra,' said Rosamund, pointing to them in turn. 'This is Muriel Hatherley, and this is Geraldine Challoner.'

'Only we call her "Gerry,"' put in Sheila. 'I thought you were with Jill and Naïda, Gerry?'

'Jill and Naïda are too busy gassing about other things,' replied Rosamund. — 'Con, Gerry is your age, so I expect she'll be in your form. Hello, here we are! Come on! Tumble out!—Cesca, it's your turn to look after Josie to-day!'

'Oh, bother! So it is,' sighed Cesca, who was a merry-faced young person of about fourteen. 'There she is!—Josie! Josie! Come along, honey!'

Josie, a dark, foreign-looking little maid of seven, ran up to them.

'This is our youngest sister,' said Rosamund. 'Where's Madge, Josie? Oh, there she is!'

Another little girl of about the same age as Josie came dancing along, and they all set off.

Helen gave a hasty glance over her shoulder, and then, seeing that Gerry was, apparently, well looked after, went off with Madeleine and Claire. Jill and Naïda had long since disappeared.

Once at the school buildings, Con took
Gerry into her charge. She led her to the
cloakroom, gave her a share of her peg, showed
her the lockers where hockey sticks and crosses
were kept, and then ushered her upstairs into
the big hall, where the first person they met
was Helen.

'Oh, there you are,' she said, catching hold
of Gerry. 'Come along; Miss Catcheside
wants to see you before prayers.—Thanks
awfully, Con.' And then she hurried Gerry
off down what seemed like an unending corridor, where girls of all sorts and sizes seemed
to be rushing hither and thither.

At the end of the corridor they came to a
door, at which Helen rapped. There was a
moment's silence, and then a voice called,
'Come in!'

Helen opened the door, pushed Gerry in
front of her, and then walked in herself. 'This
is Geraldine, Miss Catcheside,' she said.

A voice from the big roll-top desk near
the window replied, 'Oh, thank you, Helen!
That is all, dear, just now.—Come along,
Geraldine.'

And before Gerry had realised that she was
being addressed, the door closed quietly behind
Helen, and she was left alone with Miss
Catcheside.

'Come, Geraldine,' said Miss Catcheside's voice again.

And poor Gerry forced her trembling legs to carry her across the floor and round the desk.

CHAPTER VI.

MISS CATCHESIDE turned in her chair as her new pupil came to her side, and Gerry gave vent to an audible gasp. For the headmistress before her was in no smallest degree like the headmistresses she had pictured for herself. Miss Catcheside was young—very young for her responsible post—and she was a very striking-looking woman, tall and graceful, with masses of wavy, copper-coloured hair, blue eyes, and the delicate colouring which so often goes with red hair. In somewhat odd contrast were her black brows and lashes, which, with her firm mouth, gave the character to her face. She wore a white silk shirt blouse and a blue skirt, and the blue silk tie of St Peter's school. As she caught Gerry's half-scared look her lips relaxed, and she stretched out her hand with a smile.

'Frightened, are you? What fairy tales has that imp Jill been telling you about me? Silly child! I sha'n't eat you; I promise you that!'

Suddenly Gerry found herself settled comfortably in the broad window-seat, while Miss Catcheside, glancing at her watch, said, 'We've ten minutes before school, and I want to ask you one or two questions. First of all, what do you like doing best of anything?'

'Oh, playing!' returned Gerry eagerly. 'I love music more than anything else in the world!'

Miss Catcheside noted down 'musical' on the sheet before her, and then turned again to the little girl, 'And what else?'

'I like reading history,' replied Gerry; 'and I like learning poetry.'

'What about mathematics—algebra, arithmetic, and geometry? Do you like these?' asked the headmistress, noting the sensitive, mobile face of the child before her, and making her own deductions.

Gerry looked bewildered. 'I—I'm afraid I do not know algebra or geometry,' she said shyly. 'I do not like arithmetic.'

'And what about games?'

'I like croquet and La Grace,' returned Gerry.

It was Miss Catcheside's turn to gasp. Croquet she knew, and the little ones in the kindergarten played it; but La Grace was beyond her ken, although she remembered having heard her mother and aunts talking of it. 'Do you know Badminton?' she asked.

Gerry shook her head. 'No; I have not heard of it.'

'What did you do in your play-time?' asked the headmistress, realising that here she had a special case, which must be carefully dealt with.

'I sewed,' replied Gerry. 'Sometimes I read, or played at solitaire, or I went for walks.'

Miss Catcheside glanced at her watch. It was the only thing she could think of doing, and she felt she needed support of some kind. A knock at the door brought her relief, which deepened as she saw who entered in response to her 'Come in!' All that Gerry saw was a pretty girl of about twenty-three, who came hurrying across the floor.

Miss Catcheside turned to her with a smile of welcome. 'Miss Hamilton, I am so glad to see you! This is Geraldine Challoner. She has never been to school before, but I think she will be in your form. Will you ask Miss Hildreth to take it for you with hers after prayers, so that you can examine her? And——' The voice lowered, and Gerry turned to examine the

books in the bookcase with a feeling that the
ensuing conversation was not intended for her
ears. As it was in Italian, however, it would
not have mattered if she had listened. It
finished in a minute, and then Miss Catcheside
turned to the little girl with a smile. 'Now,
Geraldine, go with Miss Hamilton, and I will
see you later.—Take her to Helen Trevennor,
please, Miss Hamilton; and then, after prayers,
dear'—here she turned to Gerry—'wait behind
the others.'

'Yes, Miss Catcheside,' replied Gerry shyly,
as she turned to follow the pretty mistress,
who had reached the door by this time.

'Don't worry,' said Miss Catcheside reassur-
ingly. 'You will get on all right, and it won't
be half so bad as you think.'

Then Miss Hamilton opened the door, and
there was nothing for Gerry to do but to
follow her.

Once outside, the young mistress held out
her hand. 'Come along,' she said. 'It's two
minutes before prayer-bell, and I haven't any
idea where we shall find Helen.'

'I'm here, Miss Hamilton,' said Helen's
voice behind them.

Miss Hamilton turned with a smile. 'Ah,
Helen, I am glad to see you. Please look
after Geraldine till prayers are over. She is

to wait in the hall after the others have gone, and I will come to her there. Thank you so much!' And without further ado she left them together, and sped down the corridor in search of Miss Hildreth.

Helen smiled quizzically as she watched the tall, graceful figure. Then she looked down at her small charge. 'Well, that's Hammy,' she said. 'What do you think of her, Gerry?'

'She is exceedingly pretty,' replied Gerry soberly. 'Will she be my governess?'

'My goodness, child! Don't talk of governesses, please! Call 'em form mistresses! Yes, I rather expect that "oor Jean" will have the running of you. There's the prayer-bell! Come on!'

It seemed to Gerry as she followed pretty Nell down the corridor that every one was telling her to 'come on' to-day. Suddenly they came to two open swing-doors, through which girls of every age, size, and appearance poured—girls who were tall, girls who were short; girls who were pretty, girls who were plain; thin girls and fat girls; girls with long plaits like Nell's and her own, and girls with short bobbed hair like Jill's. Gerry fancied she caught sight of that young person sitting beneath one of the windows, but she felt so bewildered that she could not be sure of anything. Girls, girls, girls! Never before had she imagined that there were so many of them in the world. Helen was greeted on all sides; she was evidently a favourite. And many were the curious glances directed at Gerry herself. Nervously she shrank from them; and then she suddenly saw Con Atherton's pretty face beaming at her.

'Oh, here you are, Con!' said Nell at the same moment. 'Just let Gerry stay with you for prayers, will you? I'll come to her after.'

'Rather!—Come on, Gerry! Heaps of room for you here.' And Con and Muriel Hatherley, who was sitting next to her, separated a little, and Gerry was pulled into the space between them by Muriel.

'Got a book?' asked the latter young lady. 'No? All right! You can share mine! Con's sharing with Mary Anderson. She left hers at home as usual! Got a head like——'

What Mary Anderson's head was like Gerry did not learn just then, for a second bell went, and Muriel ceased speaking at once. Discipline during prayers was a thing St Peter's prided itself on. Suddenly the doors at the top of the room opened and the staff appeared.

There was a rustle and a stir, and the entire school rose to its feet as Miss Catcheside took her place at the table on the dais. The other mistresses stood round behind, and then a tall girl with reddish hair and a clear-cut face, which attracted Gerry, rose from her seat near the dais and gave out the hymn. From the organ built into the wall came a volume of music, and then the hall rang with girlish voices as they sang 'Fight the Good Fight.'

St Peter's was renowned for its singing; and Miss Beddoes, head of the music staff and senior singing mistress, insisted that whatever was sung must be sung well, so that the sound of the voices, led by the choir, which stood to right and left of the dais, produced a harmony which thrilled Gerry to the depths of her impressionable little heart. The hymn was followed by a reading from the New Testament, when Claire Ashe, very much flushed and embarrassed, struggled through ten verses of the Sermon on the Mount, and then retired to her seat with an air of obvious relief. This was followed by prayers; and when they rose from their knees Miss Beddoes struck up 'Pomp and Circumstance' on the organ, and, beginning with the kinder-garten babies, they marched out to their class-rooms.

'You'll have to stay here,' whispered Con hastily. 'It'll be all right! Nell will come for you in a minute.' Then she and Muriel were gone, and Gerry found herself left alone. But only for a minute. The next Nell descended on her, and, gripping her arm, gave it a friendly squeeze.

'Buck up, kiddie!' she said. 'Hammy's very jolly, and you needn't be frightened at all.'

The entrance of Miss Hamilton at that moment prevented any further conversation, for she quickly dismissed Helen, reminding her that she was missing her algebra lesson. Then she turned to the little new girl. 'We'll go to the staff-room, Geraldine,' she said. 'Come along, dear!'

She led Gerry along the corridor and up some stone steps, at the top of which ran another corridor. All along this, on either side, were class-rooms, and from them came the buzz of voices. Miss Hamilton nodded towards the door of one. 'That's III.A,' she said; 'the form I expect you will be in. And this,' opening a door a little farther along, 'is the staff-room junior.'

She ushered Gerry into a small, sunny room, which was bright with pictures and bowls of flowers and a cheerful fire. A small table stood near the window, and at this Miss Hamilton seated herself, bidding Gerry draw up another chair to it. 'Now, Geraldine,' began the young mistress briskly when they were ready, 'what arithmetic have you done? I suppose you have got up to fractions, vulgar and decimal? Can you do proportion, or simple interest? What about percentages and square measure?'

'I—I don't know,' faltered Gerry alarmedly.

Miss Hamilton opened widely eyes brown as one of her beloved Highland burns. Then she recollected what Miss Catcheside had said to her during that three minutes' conversation in Italian: 'This is a special case. Treat her carefully.' Leaning back, she reached an arithmetic book from the snelves, and with its aid proceeded to find out how far Gerry had gone. 'Quite average,' she commented. 'Geometry and algebra I believe you don't know. What history did you use, child?'

'Mrs Markham, and Little Arthur,' replied Gerry, with a horrible feeling that Miss Hamilton would be surprised. In point of fact that young lady had much ado to keep her countenance as she asked, 'Is that all?'

'Well, I read other books,' replied Gerry.

'What books?'

'Oh, *The Four Georges*, and *The Rise and Fall of the Roman Empire*, and somebody's *William the Silent*, and——'

'That will do, thank you,' interrupted Miss Hamilton hastily. 'What about French?'

Gerry shook her head. 'I didn't have any books. Mademoiselle Mailenne just made me read and write English into French.'

'H'm! And geography?' inquired Miss Hamilton, biting her lips furiously.

Poor Gerry! Instinctively she felt that the books she had used were all wrong. Miss Hamilton was a kind-hearted girl, and had she realised what the child was feeling she would have made even more strenuous efforts to control herself. But the climax came when she inquired, more in fun than anything else, for she did not believe it possible in the twentieth century, 'And did you use *Magnall's Questions*, too?'

'Ye-yes,' faltered Gerry.

'You did! Good gracious!'

Miss Hamilton was silent for a moment with sheer wonder. The tears came into the child's eyes. Oh, how terribly old-fashioned she must seem, she who had never done any algebra, or geometry, or physical geography, and who had been taught out of such a book

as *Magnall's Questions*! Would Miss Hamilton despise her? she wondered. What would
she say next?

'Geraldine, will you write me a composition
on "Sunday"?' came the pretty Scottish
accents.

Paper and pencil were placed before her,
and while Miss Hamilton corrected English
grammar exercises, the little new girl did her
best with the composition.

The sound of the bell brought them up
sharply, and Miss Hamilton stretched out her
hand for the essay. She glanced at the sheet of
pretty Italian handwriting, and then she smiled.
'Your writing is beautifully clear, Geraldine!
Well, dear, you can come to III.A for the
present, and I will see Miss Catcheside about
you at break. I think I will keep you, if she
will allow it. Most of your work seems to be
on an average with ours; and you must get
some one to coach you with maths. Now,
come along!' And with this she rose and
led Gerry out into the corridor, where mistresses and girls were hurrying to and fro.
At the door of III.A stood Con Atherton and
Muriel Hatherley. Miss Hamilton left her
late victim with them, and ran down the
corridor to speak to a tall, severe-looking
lady in pince-nez, whom Gerry later got to

know as the senior maths. mistress, Miss Motley.

'Are you with us?' questioned Muriel eagerly.

'Yes,' replied Gerry.

'Oh, good!   Come in!—Girls, this is Gerry Challoner, who is with us.'

CHAPTER VII.

GERRY'S INITIATION.

IMMEDIATELY there was a silence which could be felt, and twenty-two pairs of eyes fixed themselves on Gerry as Con and Muriel escorted her in triumph to a vacant desk near theirs.

'It's geography next,' said Muriel.—'Mary, you go and root out an atlas from somewhere, will you?—And, Lillie Tomson, haven't you got some loose paper? Mine's all used up.—But here's a pencil, Gerry! And I know——'

'Muriel Hatherley, may I ask why you are speaking?' said a cold voice from the doorway.

Gerry turned round with the others, and there stood a tall, cold-eyed lady, who fixed poor Muriel with a basilisk air.

'May I further inquire,' continued the lady, 'why you children are not in the geography room?—No; no excuses!' as Muriel opened her mouth.—'Get your books, and come along at once!—Muriel, you may take a detention!'

But this was more than Gerry could bear. Clasping slender hands, and with deep distress in every feature, she made a step forward, and said, 'Pardon me, madam, but indeed the fault is mine, and not Muriel's. She was being so kind as to assist me.'

There was a universal gasp. Miss Kennedy, the geography mistress, was held in awe by every one. It was even whispered that Miss Catcheside herself stood in dread of her. Certainly no other girl in III.A would have dared to speak to her like this. The majority wondered whether Gerry would be cast forth for a week, or expelled altogether. To their surprise, nothing happened—or nothing much. It is true that at first Miss Kennedy stiffened, for she rather expected a joke. But it was impossible not to realise the genuineness of the child's grief, so she merely said, 'Ah! A new girl, I see! What is your name, child?'

'Geraldine Challoner,' faltered Gerry.

'Well, Geraldine, as Muriel was trying to help you, I will forgive her, and remit the punishment. But please remember for the future, girls, that speaking between lessons is not permitted. Now, come along! We have wasted nearly ten minutes of our lesson.' And with this she swept off, leaving the girls divided between amazement at the attitude she had taken up and admiration of Gerry's pluck.

However, they dared not delay, so they snatched up their books and hastened down the corridor, the little new girl between Con and Muriel, who tried to express her gratitude by squeezing the little slim hand she held. She dared not speak again.

In the geography room Gerry was held silent with wonder. Never before had she seen a room like this. The maps, which were fastened to the walls, were made not of paper, but of some hard material, and were not flat, but—well, Gerry called it 'bumpy' to herself. There were trays of some gray-green stuff on shelves at one side of the room. There were globes, too; and right along one wall ran a blackboard. So much she realised before they were all seated and Miss Kennedy began the lesson. And what a lesson it was! None of the old dry facts about Paris being the capital of France! No mention of the respective heights of Monte Rosa and Monte Viso! Not even a reference to the population!

In her own line Miss Kennedy was something of a genius. With people like III.a she preferred to work, as she said, pictorially. So her lessons were vivid and clear, with no

unnecessary statistics, and in that three-
quarters of an hour Gerry sat enthralled by
her description of southern Italy. Gone were
the walls of the class-room, the desks, the girls!
Gerry was in the olive-groves of Cosenza; in
imagination, she wandered along the narrow
streets of Naples to the beautiful bay, where
picturesque fisher-boys lazed in the golden
heat, and brown and red sailed boats of a
structure not seen in England careened along
on the blue water. More than once Miss
Kennedy glanced down at the absorbed little
face as she talked. She was accustomed to
perfect attention, but she rarely received such
rapturous reception of her lesson as this.
When the bell rang she saw the soft glow
fade out of the brown eyes as Gerry looked
round in bewildered fashion, without attempting to get up till Muriel Hatherley pulled at
her sleeve.

'Wake up, do!' whispered Con at her other
side; 'it's half-past ten break! Come along
and we'll introduce you to the others.'

Once more they hurried down the corridor
till they came to III.a, and there Miss
Hamilton awaited them. 'Come, children!'
she said impatiently. 'Be quick and put your
books away!'

Once books were put away, they marched,

in orderly fashion, downstairs, right down to the bottom of the stairs, and into a huge room, divided by curtains, where numbers of girls were already waiting about. Through the curtains Gerry caught sight of bigger girls. She thought once that she saw Claire Ashe, but she could not be sure.

'This is where we get milk and biscuits,' said Con beside her. 'Remove up to Sixth are on the other side of the curtain; we are here; and the babies have it in the little room opposite. Then we go out if it is fine. If it's wet we stay here.'

'D'you think you'll like it?' asked a brown-haired girl from the other side. 'By the way, I'm Stella Newton—I'm a twin!'

'Oh, Stella, do dry up about that ancient history!' laughed Muriel. 'Any one would think no one had ever been a twin before! Where is Sylvia, anyhow?'

'Over there, talking to Alicia,' replied Stella cheerfully. 'She's hockey fag this week to the Second Eleven. Mary Anderson was last week!'

A shout of laughter drowned the end of her sentence.

'Mary!' exclaimed Con. 'Goodness! No wonder Alicia looks so worried!'

'Poor old Mary!' chuckled Muriel. 'Ho!

ho! ho! It's too funny for anything! I thought they always contrived to give her a miss for fagging!'

'They do,' replied Stella; 'but last week Pussy sent for Nell Trevennor, and told her that Mary was to do her fair share of the fagging, and—oh, something about it being good for her character! I can't just remember what!'

'And here's the grub at last!' exclaimed a slim, fair girl who had been standing by quietly. — 'Come on, Gerry! I'm Lillie Tomson, by the way!'

'Gently, girls, gently!' said the matron, who superintended this department. 'Muriel Hatherley, why are you taking two glasses?'

'One's for Gerry Challenor, the new girl,' explained Muriel.

'Well, can't she look after herself?' returned the matron.—'Sybil Forsyth! Do be careful what you are doing, child! You are spilling milk in all directions.'

Sybil Forsyth, a small girl of Sheila's age, with wide eyes and an attractive smile, retired hastily with her glass of milk; while Muriel pulled Gerry away from the table into a corner, where they were joined by Stella and Lillie, and, a minute later, by another girl so like Stella that it was almost unnecessary for Lillie to introduce her as 'Sylvia Newton—Stella's twin.'

She was spluttering with indignation about something, and as they drank their milk and ate their biscuits Gerry was given an insight into yet one more of the manners and customs of modern school-life. 'I hate Alicia!' she began vehemently. 'She's a perfect pig! Just because Mary Anderson forgets everything isn't any reason to rag at me about putting things away and having them ready!'

'Did she rag you like that?' queried Muriel interestedly. 'How mean!'

'She called me "child," too!' went on Sylvia, who between indignation and biscuit was becoming rather incoherent. 'Child indeed! What's she, I'd like to know?'

'It's a shame!' chorused the sympathetic hearers.

'The fact of the matter,' said Con, 'is that the Fifth Formers are getting too bossy and conceited for anything. We shall be having Remove and Fourth putting on frills next if we don't look out!'

'I know!' broke in Stella. 'Let's strike!'

'Strike?'

'Yes; like the coal-miners and railwaymen! We'll say we don't do any more fagging for any one, and then they'll have to give us our terms, and——'

'Are you children going to take all day to drink your milk?' said a cold voice just behind them.

The would-be strikers turned round hurriedly.

'O—oh, sorry, Marcia!' murmured Stella; while Sylvia and Lillie nearly choked themselves in an effort to drink their milk quickly. 'I—I didn't know——'

'Then hurry up another time,' returned Marcia, whom Gerry recognised as the big girl who had given out the hymn at prayers. 'And one of you find that new child, Gerry Challoner, and bring her to Nell Trevennor in the prefects' room!' she added with a sublime disregard of Gerry's proximity.

'Please, Gerry Challoner is here,' said Con.

Marcia looked down at her. 'Oh! Are you Gerry Challenor, child? Then you'd better come with me. Nell wants you.—You others take back your glasses to the table and go outside. You ought not to be indoors now!'

There was a meek chorus of 'Yes, Marcia;' and then Gerry felt a firm hand laid on her shoulder, and she was walked off down the corridor and into a room where sat eight or ten girls, amongst whom were Claire and

Madeleine and Nell. The last-named young lady looked up as Gerry and her escort entered the room, and her eyebrows went up.

'Found her myself,' observed Marcia, obviously answering the eyebrows, 'so I brought her along with me.'

'Thanks, awfully,' replied Nell.—'Come over here, Gerry, my lamb, and tell me how you are making it.—'Scuse me, you folk, will you?'

She pulled Gerry into a corner as she spoke, and the buzz of voices which had ceased at their entrance went on again.

'How are you making it?' repeated Nell. 'Which form are you in?'

'III.A,' replied Gerry.

'Oh, "oor Jean"! That's good! The other kids decent?'

'Oh yes!' replied Gerry fervently.

'Seen anything of Jill?'

'N-no!'

'Little rotter!' commented Jill's sister dispassionately. 'Well, remember what I said. Stick it all you can. If things get too hard for you, come to me. That's all. You can git now.'

Gerry gladly availed herself of the permission, and left the room as quickly as she could; while Nell, with a feeling that she had done her duty nobly, rejoined the group by the window, and discussed the chances St Peter's had in the forthcoming hockey match with The Grange.

At the bottom of the corridor Gerry found Con Atherton awaiting her, and with her a girl whom she had not yet seen.

'This is Kitty O'Connell,' explained Con.— 'This is Gerry, Kitty. Don't you think she'll do?'

'Simply mag.!' replied Kitty enthusiastically. 'Come on, Con! Let's go somewhere quiet and tell her.'

'Without the others?' queried Con dubiously.

'Is there time to get them?'

This question was answered by the ringing of the bell, and instantly every one made a bolt for the door.

Kitty grabbed Gerry's arm, murmured hoarsely, 'Tell you later! "'Bye"!' and vanished; while Con piloted her bewildered charge back to III.A room, where Miss Hamilton awaited them.

For the next two hours Gerry found all her attention was needed as they were whisked through arithmetic and English essay. But one o'clock brought with it release, and as soon as Miss Hamilton had left the room she turned eagerly to Con, asking, 'What is it? Oh, do tell me!'

'I can't! It isn't only my secret,' returned Con. 'Come on and get ready for dinner. We'll see Kit after dinner, and she'll tell you then. We don't begin school till half-past two. Only sewing and prep. this afternoon; but I expect you'll be excused sewing to go to the stationery room for your books.'

Gerry sighed. There seemed no end to the strange duties she was meeting at every turn. She wondered if she would ever become accustomed to this life. However, she trotted obediently along to what the girls designated 'The Splasheries,' and prepared for dinner. Here she saw Jill, and essayed a smile at her. But Jill, after a most disconcerting stare, turned her back, and Gerry was left with a choking sensation in her throat. How Jill must dislike her!

Dinner was another ordeal. French only might be spoken, and to the little new girl, fresh from the perfect accent of Mademoiselle de Mailenne, the appalling pronunciation and extraordinary grammar of the majority of the girls came as an unpleasant shock. The girls themselves stared when the new girl in rapid, fluent French replied to Miss Kennedy's questions, and even Miss Kennedy herself

looked startled. But at length the meal came
to an end, and Con and Kitty took possession
of her, and with furtive glances round led her
rapidly down into a little hollow under the
stairs, where six girls were already awaiting
them.

CHAPTER VIII.

THE SECRET SOCIETY.

KITTY looked them over with an air of calm authority which, had Gerry but known it, was modelled on Marcia's. 'Where's Mary Anderson?' she asked. 'And Olive Purvis?'

'Mary's forgotten to come,' replied Muriel with a giggle, 'and Olive's gone to find her. Isn't she the *limit*?'

'This is Gerry Challoner,' said Kitty, without further comment on the absent Mary. —'These are Leo Fairless, Gwen Compton, Myfanwy Tudor, and Tessa Donati. Lillie's in your form, so you'll know her.—The Twins can't come,' she added to the others. 'Sylvia has a music lesson, and Stella is being ragged by Pussy. Mademoiselle reported her.'

'Reported her? What on earth for?' asked the girl Kitty had called Gwen, whose well-cut face and short red curls reminded Gerry of Marcia.

'Verbs, I believe,' replied Kitty. 'I must say Stella's asked for it; and Mademoiselle was furious this morning—wasn't she, Tess?' she added, turning to the slim, dark-eyed child she had addressed as Tessa.

Tessa shrugged her shoulders. 'Mademoiselle lost her temper,' she said. 'But it is as you say, Kitty; Stella did not know anything! Here are Mary and Olive,' she went on. 'Now we can begin.'

'Come on, Mary!' said Kitty impatiently. 'Wherever have you been all this time?'

'I'm sorry; I forgot,' replied Mary meekly, a reply which was received with much merriment.

'Mary would forget her head if it was loose,' laughed Lillie.

'She'll forget her own name some day!' rejoined Muriel.

'Oh, never mind ragging!' interrupted Kitty impatiently. 'We haven't time for it.— Gerry, we're going to let you join our society, but you've got to promise and vow you'll tell nobody about it! Honour bright!'

'Oh, I will tell no one,' replied Gerry in her quaint, old-fashioned way.

'All right, then! Well, every one is down on the Middle School, because they say we are idiots. The only people they condescend to approve of are Remove and IV.A. But we're going to show them that we won't be sat on! So all us here and the Twins have made a society, and we're going to show them what we can do, and that we're not going to be treated like anything. And first of all we're going to have a play. Con wrote it, and Tessa is making the music for the songs. We were one character short. We wanted a haughty princess. Will you be her? It's an awfully nice part!'

Gerry had listened gravely to this heated, though ungrammatical, speech, and she now opened her eyes widely. 'You want me to be in your society and your play?' she said surprisedly. 'How good of you! I appreciate your great kindness so much! I thank you for it?'

If Kitty had surprised her, she more than surprised the other girls.

'Goodness!' gasped Gwen. 'D'you always talk like that?'

Gerry flushed, and looked distressed. Tessa came over to her, and slipped an arm through hers. 'But that is how I like to hear English spoken,' she said in her pretty foreign accents. 'I have lived in England only two years, Gerry, and I do not like the English slang. In Sorrento, where I lived before, my English governess spoke like you.'

'Oh, never mind that now!' interposed

Kitty hastily.—'See, here's your part, Gerry. When can you learn it? We have a rehearsal on Wednesday.'

'I will endeavour to know it by then,' replied Gerry.

'Good!—Now let's get on to the other business! Look here, you people, I'm getting fed-up with the way the Second Eleven fag us! They ragged Sylvia all ends up about the hockey.—Your fault, Mary!' And she grinned at Mary, who grinned placidly back.

'Well, how are we going to stop it?' queried Gwen doubtfully.

'We'll go on strike, of course!' replied Kitty calmly.

'Go on strike?'

'I say, what a scheme!'

'But I do not understand, Kitty!'

'What are you kids doing here?'

The conspirators started guiltily at the sound of the last voice, and got to their feet in a hurry. Marcia—for Marcia it was—eyed them severely. 'Why are you not out on the hockey-field?' she demanded.

They shuffled their feet. It is not very easy to explain to your school captain that you have been discussing the question of striking against her authority. But Marcia wanted an answer, and meant to have it.

'What have you been doing? — Kitty O'Connell, you're the oldest here. Please answer my question—at once!'

'We—we were only talking,' mumbled Kitty, turning very red. 'That's all, Marcia!'

'Well, do your talking outside, please,' replied Marcia. 'Go along, all of you; and don't let me catch you here again!'

There was nothing for it but to obey, and they filed meekly out under Marcia's severely disapproving glance. But once they were out of her sight they rallied together, and vowed vengeance until the bell rang, when they made a dash for their form rooms, only to be caught up by the captain once more and made to walk properly.

The rest of the day passed like a dream to Gerry. While the others were doing needle-work, she was escorted by Madeleine Carew to the stationery room, where that young lady proceeded to enter her name in a ledger, and then gave her piles of new books. She got a history book, two geographies, an arithmetic, a grammar, an atlas, a geometry, an algebra, a copy of Lamb's *Tales from Shakespeare*, a French grammar, a copy of *Le Chien du Capitaine*, a Latin grammar, and a pile of exercise books. Into all of these she had to gum a label, and on the label she had to write

her name, while Madeleine wrote down the
titles of the books and number of exercise
books in the ledger. Then blotting-paper,
pencils, rubber, and a pen were added, and as
the big girl blotted the last item the bell rang.

'Run along now!' she said briskly. 'Prep.
now! Mind you keep your books tidy, and
get the text-books backed! Jill Trevennor
will show you how to do them.'

Gerry felt very sure that Jill would do
nothing of the kind; but she could scarcely
say so to Madeleine, so she merely began
piling the books together. Madeleine watched
her for a moment.

'Here, you can't carry all these yourself!'
she said. She got up and opened the door
of the room. Jill happened to be passing at
the moment, and Madeleine called her. 'Jill
Trevennor, come and help Gerry Challoner
to carry her books to III.A room. And while
I remember, please see that she brings them
to-morrow properly backed!'

Jill dared not refuse outright; she stood
in too great awe of Madeleine, who possessed
a reputation for sarcasm second to none in
the school. So she took the books the prefect
gave her without a word, but with a scowl
which told Gerry that the senior had not
furthered her cause with the third Rectory

girl. When they reached the door of III.A, Jill gave up the books in a silence that was alarming, and Gerry finally settled down to preparation with a chill feeling of dread at her heart. When the four o'clock bell rang she started to her feet with a look of distress. Con offered a school-bag in which to carry the books home, and Muriel and she packed them in scientifically. Then they scampered down to the cloakroom, and put on their caps and coats and set off for the station. On the platform they were joined by Rosamund Atherton, and a little farther along they could see Francesca with Josie and the other little girl, whose name Gerry now learned was Madge Halloran. Jill and Naïda Ashe were talking earnestly together by the bookstall, and took no notice of them until the three big girls came up to them. They were presently reinforced by Marcia and Gwen and two or three tiny girls, who forgathered with Madge and Josie; and then the train came in, and they climbed into their carriages. Farther down, among a group of St Peter's boys, Gerry caught sight of Cecil and Bernard. But they took no notice of the girls, and presently she forgot them in the interest of a new book passed round by Gwen. At Mordown the Comptons—Marcia and Gwen were sisters, as Gerry had surmised—got out with them, and, seeing Gerry's surprise, Gwen explained. 'We often spend the week-end with Aunt Gwennie in Dawding. She lives there. But we live three miles from Mordown, really. The trap will be waiting for us at the inn. They don't come down to the station except in bad weather, because mummie likes us to have the walk. I say, where's Jill gone to?' she added.

'She's in front with Sheila,' said Gerry gravely.

'Oh, so she is. Whyever didn't she wait for us? Never mind; it doesn't matter! Jill's rather high and mighty since she's been Middle School captain! Thinks she's everybody, I suppose!' and Gwen grinned in a way which was most infectious. 'Look here, Gerry,' she went on, 'if you'd like to read this book, I'll have finished it by the week-end, and you can have it for Sunday. Mummie's going to ask Nell and Jill and you to spend Saturday with us, so you won't have time for reading then. I'm so glad you've come, Gerry!'

By this time they had reached the inn, and Marcia was impatiently calling to Gwen to 'hurry up,' so she had to hurry off, with a final squeeze of Gerry's arm. But her warm-hearted friendliness left an amazingly pleasant feeling; and when they reached the Rectory, and Mrs Trevennor and Margaret anxiously asked, 'How have you got on? Do you like it? Are you happy?' Gerry was able to reply quite truthfully, 'Oh, so much —so very much!'

CHAPTER IX.

SQUALLS.

'WELL, pal, how did you get on to-day?'

Gerry lifted her head from the history she was reading over, and looked up into Paul's face with a smile. 'Oh, Paul, it was lovely —just lovely! I have some new books, and my form-mistress is called Miss Hamilton, and she is exceedingly pretty! And I have some friends, too—Con Atherton, and Muriel Hatherley, and Gwen Compton. Gwen is going to lend me a book.'

'And what about lessons?' queried Paul, sitting down on the table beside her and looking approvingly at the flushed face and sparkling eyes. 'Have they put you with Sheila, eh?'

'Oh no! Sheila is in the Junior School. I am in the Middle School,' replied Gerry with dignity.

'Bottom form?'

'No! That is III.B. I am in III.A. It's ever so far below Jill, of course,' she added wistfully. 'Jill's Remove! But I have never learned algebra, geometry, or physical geography; and I know so little Latin.'

'Jill's two years older than you,' said Jill's brother slowly. 'She's been at school ever since she was seven. This is your first term; I bet that by the end of the year you'll get your Remove double if you only buck up. As for the algebra and geometry, I'll lend you a hand there.'

'Oh, Paul, will you? Really? Oh, how kind of you!'

Paul shuffled uneasily. 'Nothing to gush about!' he grunted. 'Look here, what prep. have you left to do? If you can finish in half-an-hour, I'll give you a lesson to-night. But you'll have to buck up, because Maitland is coming up after service for a game of chess, and he'll be here by eight. Think you can manage?'

'Oh yes!' And Gerry returned to her history with a vigour which left little doubt as to her determination. It is to be feared that French grammar and English parsing were both rather scamped that night; but at the appointed time Gerry proclaimed herself ready, and Paul lifted his lazy length out of the arm-chair in which he had been lounging, reading *Mr Soapy Sponge*.

Ten minutes later Jill came into the room with her mapping-book and paints. She was looking her own impish self when she entered. An hour in her father's study with Horace and Roman history had smoothed her ruffled feathers for the time being; but the sight of the two dark heads bent over the algebra book roused all the jealousy, and the scowl came back at once.

'Paul,' she said, utterly ignoring Gerry's presence, 'I can't understand my geometry! Will you help me?'

Paul looked up with raised eyebrows. It was a new thing for Jill to ask help of him. She prided herself on her mathematical powers, and, as a rule, accepted help from no one. In some ways he was rather obtuse, so he merely said, 'Well, for the love of Mike! what's happened? I'm busy just now teaching Gerry algebra, so I'm afraid I can't. Won't Larry help you if you need help?'

'Larry can't,' returned Jill briefly. 'Will you help me later?'

Paul looked worried as he replied, 'My dear kid, I can't! Maitland is coming up for chess at eight o'clock, and it's half-past seven now! I've just time to show Gerry this.'

'Paul, it's quite all right! I can manage

by myself,' said poor Gerry. She knew what Jill's present attitude meant.

'Don't be a silly kid!' replied Paul good-humouredly. 'You can't do anything of the kind!—I'll tell you what, though, Jilly,' he added; 'if you like to come down at half-past seven to-morrow, I'll give you a hand then.'

'Oh, please don't trouble yourself,' flashed Jill. 'If you won't help me now, you needn't help me at all!' And she marched out of the room, banging the door behind her.

'Heavens, what a spitfire!' ejaculated Paul. 'Gerry, my child, don't evolve a temper, what-ever you do! Now, let's see; where were we?'

'Oh, Paul,' said Gerry, twisting her fingers nervously, 'please call Jill back and help her! Oh, please, Paul, I wish you would!'

'I dare say!' retorted Paul. 'But I pro-mised you first, and I don't back out of my promises. No, no, Gerry, I offered to help her to-morrow morning, and if she doesn't like to take that, she can do without! Now, let's get back to our algebra.'

Poor Gerry! The amount of algebra she learnt that night was extremely small. Be-tween the pages of figures and letters and her eyes came Jill's face, flushed and angry, and when a tap at the door was followed by the entrance of the curate she was thankful. Paul glanced at her curiously as he said, 'Hello, Maitland! This is my pal, Gerry Challoner!'

Mr Maitland, a young and recently ordained priest, promptly stretched out an enormous freckled paw. 'Hello! How do you do? Saw you in church yesterday.'

'Thank you, I am very well,' replied Gerry sedately, as she collected her books together. 'Is it not beautiful weather?'

Mr Maitland stared, as well he might. He was not accustomed to such ceremonious behaviour from a mere school-girl, and it upset him completely.

Paul grinned to himself; while Gerry, the most unconcerned of the three, finished gathering up her possessions, and stowed the exercise books into her bag.

'What are you going to do with these?' asked Paul, touching the pile of text-books. 'Haven't they to be covered or something?'

'Yes,' replied Gerry. 'I am going now to find Nell. She will, perhaps, aid me with the work.'

'Nell's in the attic,' said Paul; 'I'll carry them up for you.—Excuse me, Maitland.— Come on, pal!'

He led her upstairs to the big attic, where

Nell, with her fingers in her ears against the wail of Cecil's viola, was struggling with Cassius's famous speech about Cæsar. She looked up with a groan as the two entered. 'Paul, do you really need me? I must get this learnt, and I haven't touched my French. It's an awful thing, too. Four pages of Madame de Sévigny to prepare!'

'Oh, may I not assist with it?' asked Gerry shyly.

Nell stared with wide-open gray eyes. 'Madame de Sévigny? My dear Gerry, isn't it rather stiff for you? Even Peggy shied at it.'

'But I read Madame de Sévigny so long ago,' explained the younger girl. 'I do not find French difficult, and I read it as well as I read English. Permit me to aid you.'

'Well, of course, if you can!'

'And, Nell,' interrupted Paul, 'you might just show Gerry how to back her books, will you? So-long!' And dropping his load on the table, he clattered off downstairs, leaving the two girls together.

And here Jill found them when she came, at her mother's behest, to fetch Gerry to supper. 'You've to come to supper,' she said, and immediately turned on her heel and ran downstairs.

Nell's face flamed with sudden anger. 'Gerry,' she said, 'Jill's behaving like a little beast to you! I am so sorry, dear.'

'Oh, Nell, it is truly all right! Perhaps Jill will make friends later on,' replied Gerry unsteadily.

'Well, come on now! I'll come for supper, too!'

And Nell slipped an arm round the younger girl as she drew her downstairs to the nursery, where supper awaited them. Margaret superintended it, for Mrs Trevennor was occupied with Geoff, who had developed a nasty cough. There was an electric feeling in the air, as though something were going to happen. Jill drank her milk and munched her biscuits in sulky silence, which even Bernard could not prevail on her to break; Cecil, who was beginning with a cold, was too tired to talk, and his eldest sister watched him anxiously. She did not want to alarm their mother, who was already sufficiently worried over Geoff, so she said nothing. Nell was turning over in her mind schemes for the reform of Jill; and Larry brought his Thucydides to table with him, and was too absorbed to pay attention to any one. Towards the end of the meal, however, he raised his head and looked across at Gerry, who was facing him.

'Can you play accompaniments?' he asked.

'W-what is it?' asked Gerry, startled at the sudden question.

'Well, in this instance it's a string quartette. Nell says you are keen on music; if you're keen, come on downstairs and try this over, will you?'

Gerry's eyes glowed like stars as she replied, 'Oh, I should so like to!—May I, Peggy?'

Margaret groaned at the name as she replied, 'Oh yes, I suppose you may!—But Cecil isn't coming, Larry! He's got to go to bed.'

'No need,' replied Larry. 'Maitland has his fiddle here.—Bear, buck up an' finish eating, will you?—You coming to listen, Jilly?'

'No!'

Her brother's eyebrows went up at this curt response; but he said nothing more to her, merely turning to Helen. That young lady shook her head decidedly. 'No can do,' she said, quoting a favourite sailor cousin of theirs. 'Run along, you three, and rejoice Paul's heart!'

'Oh, all right.—Come on, Gerry! We'll see what you can do with our dear friend Schumann.' And, catching her hands, Larry laughingly hauled her out of her chair and chased her from the room.

In the drawing-room they found the vicar

and the two young men sitting talking over the affairs of the world.

At the sight of the trio Paul's face lightened. 'Come for some music?' he said. 'Oh, good! We can try that string quartette, as every one's too busy to accompany us.'

'Except Gerry,' replied Laurence. 'She can play.—Look, here it is, Gerry! Think you can manage it?'

Gerry looked eagerly at the music which he showed her, and her face glowed with excitement. 'Oh yes; I think so, Larry!'

Paul's lips shaped themselves to a soundless whistle at her words. Margaret had shied at the music.

But the way in which the little visitor glanced over the music while they were tuning their instruments was sufficient in itself to show him that here was no mere strummer, and when they began Gerry's methods of handling it awakened a rare enthusiasm in him.

As for Gerry herself, she was far away in a wonderful world of her own, where troubles of everyday life were not, and she paid no heed to anything else. The vicar, sitting revelling in the music, glanced at her curiously. A great lover of music, and the possessor of a fine bass voice, his knowledge was considerably more than that of the usual amateur. And for a little girl of twelve to sit down and play Schumann at sight, and so well, struck him as something quite out of the ordinary. As the quartette drew to its close he held out his hand to her. 'Gerry, my child, come here!'

Gerry came at once, and he pulled her down on to his knee in the same way as he would have done Jill.

'Do you love music, girlie?'

Gerry nodded. Her heart was too full to allow her to speak.

'You have worked at it? Practised much?'

Again Gerry nodded.

'How much?' asked Paul excitedly. 'Gerry, you play wonderfully. Tell us, pal! How long have you learned?'

Gerry found her voice at last. 'I have learned since I was four,' she said. 'In the holidays I only did two hours' practice, but during term-time I used to do three, and sometimes four. I love it!'

'Gerry and Bear, you must come to bed,' said Margaret's voice at this juncture. 'Come along, dears, at once!'

'Yes, go! Good-night, my children,' said the rector, who made it a point of honour never to upset household arrangements unless

for some grave reason. As he said, ten children meant a great deal of work, and when
one of them was constitutionally delicate and
another had a tendency to croup, the only way
in which things could be run comfortably
was by every one abiding by the rules.
Bernard knew this, and made no remark, but
put his cello away ; and Gerry had been taught
instant and unquestioning obedience almost
from her earliest days. So they went off
quietly after saying 'Good-night.'

'Jill's in bed already,' said Margaret, as
they reached Gerry's door.

'Don't let Cecil talk, Bear, there's a dear !
He's rather inclined to be "chesty" to-night ;
but I don't want mother to know, as she's
worried over Geoff, and I've rubbed him
thoroughly, and put thermogene on.'

'All right,' replied Bernard. ''Night, old
bean !—'Night, Gerry ! You play rippingly,
my kid !'

'You'll be quick, won't you, Gerry ?' said
Margaret, as she turned up the light. 'I'll
go and set your bath running while you
undress.'

She vanished before Gerry could reply, and
the little girl made all the speed she could.
Twenty minutes later Margaret was tucking
her in, and lighting the night-light which

Mrs Trevennor, on learning that the child was afraid of the dark, had promptly established in the room. 'Good-night, sweetheart,' murmured the older girl. Sleep well! Mother may come in later on to see you; she generally goes the rounds.'

'Good-night,' replied Gerry drowsily. She was so warm and comfy, so deliciously warm and comfy.

CHAPTER X.

A MIDNIGHT BATTLE.

GERRY was dreaming. She thought that she was walking along the school corridor with Paul, trying to find her form room, as he had left his violin there, and now couldn't remember how to get to the room. The worst of it was that she couldn't remember either, and Jill kept coming just in front of them and mocking at them; and then an earthquake suddenly happened. Everything rocked to and fro; the walls were falling, and——

At this juncture Gerry woke up to find that some one was shaking her violently. As the sleep mists cleared out of her eyes she recognised the face above her, and sat up with a start. 'Jill!' she said. 'Oh, are you not cold? Come in beside me!' She threw back the clothes as she spoke, and moved to one side to make room.

Jill threw out her hands with a little contemptuous gesture. 'Come in beside you!' she said, albeit in low tones, for she had no wish to wake Margaret, whose bedroom was farther along the landing. 'Come in beside you! I'd—I'd sooner freeze to death! I hate you! I loathe you! I wish you'd never come! You've spoilt everything! Paul would have helped me to-night if you hadn't been there! I s'pose you think you're awfully clever 'cos he calls you "pal"! Well, you're not! You're a nuisance, and one extra! Because of you, Sheila can't go with us to the Comptons' on Saturday! She always went before, but now you've done her out of the invitation! Because of you, Larry and Nell are being beastly to me! They never were before you came, and it's all your fault! And I hate you! Hate you! Hate you! Go away to your old aunts! No one wants you here, you—you snake in the grass!' Here Jill paused for sheer lack of breath, and stood with her chest heaving and her eyes flashing stormily.

At first Gerry had shrunk from the lash of her tongue; but she was very proud, and though the tears were not far off, she forced them back. Jill should never see her cry. 'I'm sorry about Sheila, Jill——' she began.

But Jill turned on her in a flash. 'Don't call me "Jill"! I'm "Gillian" to you! Sorry about Sheila? Oh, you can say so!

If you're really sorry, you won't go!
But it's all talk! I know! Why did you
come? We were happy before you came!
You've spoilt everything—you, with your
stupid curls, and your idiotic frocks, and the
mad way you talk! You might have come
out of the ark! Everybody's laughing at you,
and I'm glad, glad, glad! I hope they'll go
on laughing! I'll laugh with them! And
you can go and tell that I said so! Sneak!'

'I'm not a sneak! I never tell tales!'
retorted Gerry, now almost as angry as Jill.
'I don't care if you do hate me, either!'

'Don't you? Then I'll make you care!
I s'pose you think just 'cos you can play a
little that you're everybody! You're not!
I'll make Betty and Sheila, and Geoff and
Bear, hate you, too!'

'I don't care! You can't make Paul hate
me! He likes me! He calls me "pal"! He
doesn't call you that!'

'He doesn't need to! I'm his sister! It's
only a fad! Paul's always getting them!
He'll get tired of you presently, and drop
you, and then you'll be sorry! Think he's
going to fag himself after a kid like you?
Not him.'

'Well, I'll wait till he does!' Gerry was
thoroughly roused now. 'And if you hate

me, I'll hate you, so there, Gillian Trevennor! Just 'cos you're captain of the Middle School you think you can do everything!' This, with a remembrance of Gwen Compton's words. 'You can't! You're only a little girl, after all—and a very horrid one, too!'

By this time Gerry was out of bed as well, and was standing on the floor, facing Jill. There was something almost comical in the scene, as the two stood there with the moonlight gleaming on their flushed faces and clenched hands. Jill's hair was all on end; Gerry's curls were scattered over her shoulders. They wagged their heads ferociously at each other as they spoke.

'Oh, am I?' gasped Jill, now almost too furious to speak clearly. 'Am I?'

'Yes, you are! You're a silly, bad-tempered, spoilt little girl!'

How in the world they managed to waken no one was a mystery never solved. But they did attract some one's attention. Paul had stayed up after the others had gone to bed, in order to read. As the clock chimed two he decided, with a yawn, that he had better go upstairs. Accordingly he put his book away, turned out the light, and took up his electric torch, so that he should not fall over anything in the dark. As he ascended the stairs his quick ears caught the sounds of battle proceeding from Gerry's room. He raced up the last two or three stairs, and opening the door, went in. By that time the bedclothes had somehow or other joined the combatants on the floor, and at first all he could see was a heaving mass, from which gasps and sobs and smothered ejaculations came. Setting down his torch, he sought for matches and lit the gas. Then he shut the door in case his mother should be disturbed, and bending over the struggling heap, he managed to disentangle it. Pulling the bed-clothes away, and throwing them into a corner, he dragged the opponents apart, and set them on their feet, holding an arm of each firmly. At first he nearly smiled, they looked so ludicrous. Tears of rage and dust from the floor had streaked both crimson countenances finely. The frilled collar of Gerry's night-dress had got torn; one of Jill's sleeves was half out of the arm-hole. One of Gerry's fists had got home on Jill's nose, and in addition to dirt her face was streaked with blood. Gerry herself had a large swelling on one temple, where Jill had bumped her against the leg of the bed. Then he grew serious as he saw the hatred gleaming in the eyes of both.

'You'd better come to the bathroom,' he

said briefly. 'Come quietly, unless you want to disturb the mater!'

They went. Paul's grasp was none too gentle, and something in his manner helped to calm them slightly. With the aid of a sponge and hot water he contrived to get them clean, and then he turned to his sister. 'Go and get into a fresh night-dress and get into bed! I'm coming to you presently.— Gerry, go to bed, too! Oh, I forgot! You pulled all the clothes on to the floor!—Jill, go and help Gerry to make the bed again!' He marched them back to the bedroom, and superintended the making of the bed. Then remarking, 'I'm coming back presently,' he led Jill upstairs, with a grim expression on his face which rather scared that young lady, now rapidly coming to her senses. 'I'll give you two minutes to change,' he said; 'then I'm coming in. Be quick!'

Jill was quick! When he entered two minutes later she was lying in her little bed by the window. He glanced at Nell, placidly sleeping the sleep of the just and weary, and then pulled the clothes round the younger girl. Jill's arms went up round his neck, but he quietly loosened them.

'No, thank you, Gillian! You have violated the hospitality of our house, and I'm ashamed of you! I will see you in the morning at half-past seven. Good-night!' And with this he left her to sob herself heart-brokenly to sleep.

Downstairs, he found Gerry crying pitifully. The events of the day had worn her out, and she was rather inclined to be hysterical. He got her some water, and then sat by her till she was quieter. But he would hear no explanations. 'Your duty now is to go to sleep,' he said quietly. 'I will see you both in the morning, and you can tell me everything then. Now, stop crying, like a good girl!'

Eventually, at three o'clock, he tumbled into bed, having seen Gerry well on the way to Slumberland, and slept soundly until the alarm-clock went off at seven.

Bernard was the first to rouse up. He got out of bed grumbling, and, snatching up his towels, made his way to the bathroom, where he collided with his twin, who was just coming out. 'Hello!' he said. Then, as he saw her disfigured face, 'I say, what on earth have you been up to? Your nose is twice its usual size! Been scrapping with Nell?'

'Mind your own business,' snapped Jill, 'and leave me to mind mine!'

She marched off upstairs, leaving him gasping. It was rare indeed that Jill turned on her beloved twin. But Paul was already coming downstairs, so he bolted himself in and raced through his ablutions. Later, while practising his cello in the greenhouse, he tried to think what had gone wrong, but could come to no satisfactory conclusion.

Meanwhile Paul had gone to the study, which he knew would be unused at that time of the day, and thither came to him Jill and Gerry. Both looked tired and rather white, which was scarcely to be wondered at. Gerry had contrived partly to hide the lump on her right temple with her hair; but Jill's nose was most conspicuous, and it was with difficulty that he could restrain a smile. However, he contrived to keep his countenance and greet the pair gravely. 'Good-morning! Shut the door, please, Jill! I don't want any one to know more about last night's affair than we can help! Thank you. Now, come here!'

They came, albeit unwillingly. Jill was still cut to the heart by Paul's refusal of her kiss last night, and Gerry felt frightened of him in this new guise.

'Now, I want an explanation,' he said seriously, when they stood on either side of him. 'Jill, you first!'

Jill stood sullenly silent, her lips in a thin line.

'I am waiting, Jill!' Paul's voice was very quiet, but quite relentless, and Jill realised that he meant to have his explanation.

'I detest you!' she said.

'Don't be so childish, Gillian! I want your explanation. Last night you broke all the laws of hospitality, and I want to know why you did so! Please tell me!'

Gerry looked at Jill. Something told her that the older girl was very miserable, and her generous little heart prompted her to try to help Jill; but the demon of pride, which was her besetting sin, stilled the prompting, and she stood quite still.

'Gillian!' Jill jumped. She had never heard Paul like this. 'I intend to have an explanation if we stay here all day! Do you realise that?'

Yes, she realised it. But Paul would have been better advised to take a different tone. Jill was far more easily led than driven, and in her present mood she was too furious to care much what happened.

'Very well,' she flung at him, 'I hate her! I hate her because you like her, and she's spoiling everything! I——'

'That will do, Gillian!—Now, Geraldine, your explanation.'

Gerry hung her head. 'I—I didn't like

her, and I went for her!'—which was the
first piece of slang any one had heard from
her lips.

But Jill, though proud and passionate, was
eminently straight and fair. 'I hit her first,'
she said. 'I started it!'

Here was Paul's opportunity. If he had
only forgotten his attitude as judge and had
petted her, Jill's defences would have broken
down, and the chances are that much that
happened, and a great deal of the heartache
which was to come, might have been averted.
But he, too, was very proud, and he felt furiously angry that any sister of his should so
forget herself as to treat a guest as Gerry had
been treated. As for Gerry, that little speech
of Jill's killed the pride in her heart.

'I—I'm sorry, Paul,' she said, looking
wistfully at her enemy.

Paul smiled and took her hand. Then he
looked at Jill expectantly. But his cold ac-
ceptance of her last words had frozen Jill, and
she stood dumbly there. 'Won't you say you
are sorry, Jill?' he asked her. But it was too
late. Jill shook her head. She felt that if
she spoke she must cry. Paul got up with a
disappointed look.

'Then, Gerry, since Gillian won't apologise
to you, I must! I am exceedingly sorry that

any member of our family should have behaved so to you.   Please forgive her!'

Perhaps, if he had let matters alone even then, Jill might have given in.   But that last speech settled everything.   Henceforth it was to be war to the knife, and Jill was no mean opponent.

The breakfast-bell ringing just then brought the interval to a close.   Paul put his arm round Gerry's shoulders.   'Come along, pal!' he said cheerily.   'We'll make a rush and bag seats together, shall we?'   And, still laughing, he drew her from the room without another glance at Jill.

CHAPTER XI.

JILL was utterly and completely miserable. Her mother was grieved at her attitude to their little guest; Nell and Larry frankly told her she was behaving abominably; Paul took no more notice of her than if she had not been there; and even her beloved twin asked her why on earth she could not be sensible and make it up. 'It's not like you to hang on to a grudge, Jilly,' he said reprovingly.

Jill lifted the most temper-struck face he had ever seen. 'Did any of them ask you to speak to me?' she demanded.

'No; don't be a fool, Jill! You ought to know them better!'

'Then leave it alone! It's no affair of yours, is it? Then keep out of it! Go away, and leave me alone!'

Bernard went. As he afterwards said, 'When a chap's told to clear out, he clears out if he's got any sense.'

Once he was gone, Jill's head went down on her arms, and her English essay was blotted by some of the bitterest tears she had ever shed. But, miserable as she was, she refused to make it up. The demon of pride was having things very much his own way just now where she was concerned. When Friday came, and Gerry, mindful of Jill's words of that stormy Monday night, tried to back out of going to the Comptons', her enemy watched her with a sneer, which made things difficult.

Mrs Trevennor, however, would not hear of it. 'Stay at home and let Sheila go instead? Certainly not! The invitation expressly said you, and I want you to go, dearie. Don't you like the Comptons? Has Marcia been too high-handed lately?'

'I scarcely ever see Marcia,' replied Gerry. 'No, it isn't that. It's just—just——'

'Have you squabbled with Gwen?'

'Oh no! Gwen's a dear! We are chums, you know.'

'Then there can be no possible reason, and I want you to go. Don't trouble about Sheila. I am inviting Allegra and Josie Atherton over to tea, and they and Geoff will have a tea-party with their dollies.'

'Is that the Athertons you are talking about, mummie?' asked Nell at this juncture, looking up from her Latin. 'Rosamund Atherton asked me if Jill and Gerry might

spend the week-end there next week. I
think Mrs Atherton is going to write to you
about it.'

'That will be nice!' And Mrs Trevennor
smiled at Gerry. 'You will like that, won't
you, Gerry?'

But Gerry felt dubious. She would have
enjoyed being with the Athertons; but with
Jill in her present mood, she was not so sure
that it would be pleasant. No more was said,
but next morning Jill woke up with a bad
cold and a sore throat. No one could imagine
how she had got it, but there she was, croaking
almost as badly as Cecil, who was in the
night nursery recovering from a bronchial
attack. Poor Mrs Trevennor rushed upstairs
on hearing from Nell of Jill's sudden illness,
and promptly decreed that the invalid must
spend the day in bed. 'I can't think how
you have caught cold, Jill,' she said in worried
tones; 'you get it so seldom!'

But Jill could have told. She had no desire
to go to the Comptons' under existing circumstances. Marcia and Nell were great chums,
and Gerry and Gwen were always together.
The only other girl in the Compton family
was Doria, who was twenty-two, and engaged;
and there were no boys save Arthur, who
was Larry's chum, and much too grand to pay

attention to Larry's fourteen-year-old sister.
And, in any case, the two were playing in a
Rugger match in the afternoon. So, rather
than go, naughty Jill had got out of bed at
twelve o'clock in the night, and had paraded
about the house in night-dress and bare feet;
and here she was in the morning, with a
temperature and a sore throat.

It was a rare thing indeed for Jill to be
ill, and after breakfast she had a stream of
visitors. Margaret had attended to her, and
she had just finished setting the room to
rights when a tap heralded Nell's advent.
'Hello!' she said. 'You're a nice one, aren't
you?'

'Hello!' croaked Jill.

'Well, you've spoilt yourself for the Comptons! Poor old Jilly!'

Jill said nothing. She couldn't very well
tell Nell that her words were literally true;
so she just lay there, feeling very uncomfortable; and presently Nell got up and went
away. The next visitor was Bernard. He
looked quite scared when he saw her, and
was so clumsily tender and concerned that he
upset Jill, who was feeling physically wretched,
so that she burst into tears and cried till he
flew for his mother. She, after one glance
at her little daughter's flushed cheeks and

heavy eyes—the tears had ceased during his absence—stopped all visitors, and forbade any one but Margaret to enter the room. 'If she isn't better when the doctor comes, I think I'll ask him to look at her,' she said to the rector in troubled tones. 'She is so thoroughly unlike herself, Arthur.'

The rector sighed. Events of the past few days had bothered him considerably. Dr Nuttall had hinted that in view of Cecil's continued delicacy it was unwise that he should remain in England during the winter months. But whence was money to come to send him abroad? True, Larry and Bear were costing him nothing in the way of education, since both held valuable scholarships. But the three girls at school were a fairly heavy expense; Geoff would have to be entered for the St Peter's Preparatory at Easter; Paul was earning very little; and the living at Mordown was not a large one. How were affairs to be arranged? Cecil could not go alone; his mother would have to go with him. Here the rector suddenly remembered a quotation from his favourite, Thomas à Kempis: 'Seek not much rest, but much patience.'

He turned to his wife with a reassuring smile. 'Don't worry, Meg! I'll go up and

see her myself. But I'm inclined to think
it's simply the combined results of bad temper
and cold. She's been pretty miserable all
this week, poor kiddie! I'll soon put her to
rights!' And with that he ran upstairs.

Half-an-hour later he came down with the
news that Jill was sleeping peacefully; and
then he turned his attention to seeing that
Gerry and Nell were well wrapped up, for
the October days were very chilly. Larry
came out to the trap, carrying an attaché-
case with his football kit.

'Drive carefully, old man!' warned his
father. 'Firefly is very fresh.'

'Right oh, pater!' he replied, as he gathered
up the reins.—'Here, kid, keep your hands
to yourself!' for Gerry had suddenly gripped
his arm in an access of nervousness.

'Don't let them give her any oats at the
Comptons',' said the rector.

'All right!—Ready, Nell?—Ta-ta, every
one! We'll be back by eight at latest.'

They were off, Firefly going along the road
at a smart pace. Larry was a good driver;
and Firefly, though fresh, did not pull unduly
at the reins.

They arrived at Beckwith Manor, the Comptons' house, in less than half-an-hour, and there
they were greeted by Mrs Compton, who made

Gerry think of Marcia grown middle-aged and motherly. She inquired for Jill, and on learning of the young lady's indisposition, promptly insisted that the boys must leave some grapes for her when they drove in to the station in the afternoon. Then she turned to Gerry. 'And so this is Gerry? I've heard so much about you from Gwen, dear, that I feel as though you were an old friend. I hope we shall often see you here; but don't let my naughty baby lead you into mischief. Here they come!' she added as Marcia and Gwen came racing round the corner of the house. 'They were feeding the hens when you came.'

Marcia, captain of the school, seemed, some-how, to be a different person from Marcia at home. The first Marcia was a very dignified person, who called you 'child,' and ordered you about, and generally suppressed you. The second was very charming, and addressed you as 'Gerry,' and asked if you wouldn't like to come and see the horses at once. Gwen, of course, was just Gwen, as always. She tucked her arm into Gerry's, and led the way to the stables, chattering excitedly, while the two big girls followed more slowly. In the stables Larry and Arthur Compton were seeing about Firefly's welfare; and Marcia, after greeting Larry, introduced her brother, 'just as though I were a grown-up!' thought Gerry.

Arthur shook hands; but he could scarcely be expected to bother much about a small girl of twelve, and presently he and Larry went off, leaving the girls to themselves. It was very nice of Marcia to be so friendly; but Gerry and Gwen had so much to discuss that it was rather a relief when she and Nell sauntered off, leaving the younger girls to their own devices.

'Let's go to the home wood,' suggested Gwen. 'I've heaps to ask you, and the gong won't go for another hour.'

So they wandered out of the stable-yard and through the kitchen-garden into the home wood, a delightful place, carpeted with autumn leaves, and with the blue October sky peeping down through the bare branches of the trees.

The two little girls wandered up and down the narrow paths with their arms round each other, talking nineteen to the dozen.

'I think *The Princess Mederia* is going to be splendid, don't you?' said Gwen presently. 'You really are splendidly haughty, Gerry! How d' you do it?'

'Oh, I watch Alicia Brett,' explained Gerry. 'And you are a lovely Prince, Gwen!

And won't Sylvia look beautiful as the Princess Mederia?'

'Gorgeous!' agreed Gwen enthusiastically. 'I think Con's awfully clever to have written it! Don't you?'

'Yes, awfully!' From which it will be seen that even just a week at school had made a change in Gerry's vocabulary.

Marcia and Nell saw them through the trees. 'I wonder what these kids are talking about,' laughed Marcia.

'Something very serious, judging from the rate they are going at!'

'Oh, it will be some nonsense or other,' replied Nell. 'By the way, have you heard of Kitty O'Connell's secret society?'

'My dear girl, I knew about it ages ago!' returned Marcia. 'They took to holding meetings under the stairs, you know, and I had to turn them out. I don't think there's any harm in it. Kitty's a good deal of an idiot, but she's perfectly straight, and so long as it doesn't annoy Us, I don't mind it! Gwen's in, of course!'

'So is Gerry. She's awfully keen!'

'I like Gerry,' said Marcia thoughtfully. 'She's a nice kid. Miss Beddoes thinks she ought to do something with her music.'

'Yes, I know; which reminds me, it's the

middle of October, and we haven't made any arrangements for the hockey club concert. I want it to be extra specially good this year!'

'I vote we go in and draw up a programme,' replied Marcia decidedly. 'Each one of the teams must supply some items, you know. And the choir can give us a part-song or two.'

The two big girls sauntered slowly back through the trees, and presently reached the Manor, where they turned in and went to the schoolroom, a bright, cheery apartment, which was theirs entirely. Here they encountered Doria, who was sitting darning Gwen's stockings.

'Hello, Nell!' she said. 'What happened to the match for this afternoon? I just heard this morning that it was scratched.'

'They've got mumps at The Grange,' explained Nell. 'An awful bore, isn't it? Still, I s'pose it can't be helped!'

'And when is the hockey concert coming off?' Doria had been captain at St Peter's five years ago, and she still took a deep interest in the welfare of the teams. Marcia was only an average player, but Gwen was brilliant, and Doria herself was a county reserve. Nell was, therefore, glad to seize the opportunity of discussing one or two knotty points with her, and the time passed so rapidly that all were surprised when the luncheon-bell rang.

After luncheon the boys set off for the station; and Mr Compton, a big, burly man, with twinkling eyes like Gwen's, offered to take them all out for a drive in the motor. 'I've got to go to Nevin,' he said. 'What do you say to coming with me, hey?—How would you like it, Gerry?'

'I do not know,' replied Gerry. 'I have never ridden in a motor-car.'

'No time like the present to begin, then! You can't begin any sooner, can you?—Well, dear, what about it?'

Mrs Compton laughed aloud. 'Where is the use of asking me, when you know you intend us to go? As a matter of fact, I'm very glad!—Dorrie, are you coming?'

'Yes, if I can pack in,' replied Doria.

'Good!' said Mr Compton. 'Then that's settled!'

And so it was. Immediately there was a general scramble upstairs, and the two visitors were wrapped up in warm coats. Then they were all packed into the car—Nell and Marcia in front; Mrs Compton and Doria, with Gerry and Gwen cuddled between them, in the tonneau.

Oh, that drive! To Gerry it seemed the

nearest approach to flying that she could have imagined. As she sat with her flying curls, and wind-flushed cheeks, and glowing eyes, she made a charming picture. Marcia, glancing back, noted it, and drew Nell's attention to it. 'She shall come in the play as a pixie,' she said. 'Just look, Nell! Why, the kid's quite lovely, isn't she?'

'Daddy says,' returned Nell, 'that her father was one of the handsomest boys imaginable, and her mother was fairy-like, she was so lovely! Gerry has her features, daddy says, but she's dark like her father.'

'She'll be ripping when she's grown up,' commented Marcia. And then the talk left Gerry.

At Nevin they got out, and Mrs Compton and Doria went shopping; while Mr Compton, having put up the car at a garage, took the four school-girls to the cinema. Gerry had never seen anything like this before. Her enraptured attention drew Marcia's notice. She was sitting next to the little girl, and during one film, when the heroine seemed unlikely to get out of her difficulties, an impulse made her slip one arm round the little tense form beside her. 'It's all right, kiddie,' she whispered. 'Things will come all right in the end!'

That one action secured her a worshipper for life. Gerry cuddled up to her with a smile, which said so much that she was too shy to say, that Marcia felt startled. She was accustomed to adoration—the school captain generally comes in for a large supply of that—but never, in all her eighteen years, had she encountered such whole-hearted worship. As for Gerry, she mentally placed Marcia beside her other idol, Margaret Trevennor.

After the cinema they all met the shoppers, and went to a café for tea, and then home again, where the evening was spent in round games, and Gerry was initiated into the mysteries of 'Donkey' and 'Up, Jenkins.' When, finally, they all climbed into the trap to go home, she decided that this was the most eventful day of her life.

But there was still another adventure before her.

CHAPTER XII.

'ISN'T Firefly awfully fresh?' asked Nell, as they went down the drive, after saying 'Good-bye' to the Comptons.

'Not more 'n usual!' grunted Laurence, who secretly was feeling dismayed at the way the mare was prancing along on three legs. 'She always pulls a bit when she is going home. So glad to get back to her stable. Aren't you, old girl?'

The 'old girl' merely laid her wicked ears back, and shied at something she pretended to see in the shadows. She had had a long rest, and, since Larry had forgotten to say anything about it to the Comptons' groom, a good feed of oats. In consequence, she felt brimful of high spirits and mischief; and if the drive home lacked incident—well, it wouldn't be her fault! Larry pulled her back to the right side of the road and set his teeth grimly. He knew that even now it was as much as he could do to keep the mare in hand. If they met anything which really startled her, he doubted if he would be able to keep her from bolting. But it was no use alarming the girls, so he said nothing, and for five minutes Firefly went on her way in her dancing manner, but still quite quietly. Then it happened! Out of the ditch, almost under Firefly's very nose, arose a figure, which even in the moment of horror Larry recognised as that of one Jem Gough, a ne'er-do-weel and a drunkard. It was more than enough for Firefly. Shying so violently that she sent the light trap half across the road, she made a snatch, got the bit firmly between her teeth, and bolted. Flinging a hasty 'Hold tight!' over his shoulder to the girls, Larry braced his feet against the front of the trap, and threw all his weight on to the reins. Nell went very white, but she kept her head. Clinging firmly to the back of the seat with one hand, she gripped Gerry with the other, holding her so tightly that later they found five black finger-prints on the little arm. At the time, however, Gerry was too terrified to feel it. When Firefly first bolted she had screamed and attempted to leap to her feet, but Nell had frustrated that intention. Then sheer terror kept her rigid, and she sat, clinging instinctively to the rail, watching hedges and

trees flash past with eyes that were dilated
and fixed. On, on they went, past cottages
and fields, beyond the turning which led to
the Rectory, down a gentle incline, over the
wide old toll bridge. Larry began to draw
his breath more easily. They were coming
to a long, steep hill. If they could only reach
it without further trouble, he knew that he
would be able to check Firefly's headlong
career. There were two turnings to be
negotiated, both of them gentle ones. Firefly
was beginning to tire; he could feel it in the
gradual command he began to have over her.
They reached the first turning, and passed it
in safety. The second was not so easy; and
now they were at the foot of the hill. The
mare was still flying, but the steep gradient
defeated her. Almost at the top she slackened
and released her hold of the bit. With a white
face Larry knew that the struggle was almost
over. When they reached the summit Firefly
stopped, and stood sweating, trembling, covered
with foam, and, turning her head, she whinnied
softly. Rallying himself, Larry backed them
down a lane, and turned her in the Mordown
direction. Now that the great strain was
over, he was feeling deathly sick; but the
girls must be got home before he could give
in, and, as nearly as he could guess, they were

still some miles away. Firefly, now completely under control, trotted meekly down
the hill, and then set off at her usual pace.
Nell, with the tears running unheeded down
her face, had Gerry in her arms, and was
trying to soothe the wild sobs which shook
the younger girl from head to foot.

It was half-past ten before they drew up
at the Rectory gate, where Mrs Trevennor
was awaiting them, Paul and Margaret by
her side.

'Hold the mare!' Larry managed to say.

Bernard, who had come racing down the
path, ran to her head, while Paul lifted Gerry
out and gave her to his mother. Nell got
down, feeling very shaky and sick, and then
Larry climbed out of the trap too. He
swayed as he reached the ground, and Paul
hurried to him. 'Are—are we all safe?' he
gasped. 'Firefly bolted!'

'My darling, quite safe!' said his mother,
who had given Gerry over to Margaret and
had taken him into her arms.

'Thank God!' he got out. The next minute
he was on the ground, utterly unconscious.

'He's fainted!' cried Paul. 'The strain's
been too much for him!—Bear, hang on to
Firefly!—Peggy, go and fetch dad!—All
right, mater; he's coming round again!

We'll have him in bed in a brace of shakes! Don't worry, dear!'

He was right. Larry's fainting fit had only been momentary. Already he had opened his eyes, and as his brother spoke he tried to sit up. 'Hello!' he said faintly. 'What's up?'

'All right, old man,' replied Paul gently. 'You turned a bit queer.'

'Oh, I remember.' Larry was now leaning back against his mother's shoulder. 'Are—are the girls all right?'

'Quite all right,' returned Mrs Trevennor. 'Here is dad, and he and Paul will help you to get to bed, darling.'

'I'm all right,' Larry assured her. Nevertheless he was thankful for the strong arms flung round him, for when he tried to stand up he found that he was very giddy. They got him into the house and on to the dining-room sofa, where he was dosed with sal-volatile, and where his mother sat beside him stroking his hair. Presently she got up and went upstairs to see after Nell and Gerry. Gerry was nearly asleep when she got there. Margaret had given her a hot bath, followed by a basin of bread-and-milk, and she was pleasantly drowsy. Mrs Trevennor kissed her tenderly; but Gerry's eyes were heavy with sleep, and it was only a few minutes later when Margaret stole quietly away.

Helen was lying in bed crying quietly to herself; while Jill, who was under a promise not to get up, made encouraging remarks from her corner. The rector's wife sat down, and took her weeping girl into her arms. For all her seventeen years, Nell cuddled down as if she had been Betty or Sheila.

'My brave little girl!' said her mother huskily. 'Larry has told me how plucky and quiet you were. He says if it hadn't been for your courage, things would have been much worse.'

Nell stopped crying from sheer surprise. 'My courage!' she repeated. 'My courage! But I didn't do anything—bar holding on to Gerry and the trap.'

'And that was the right thing to do,' replied Mrs Trevennor quietly. 'If it hadn't been for you, that poor child might have tried to jump out in her panic, and have injured herself badly, if she had not been killed.'

An unlovely sneer curled Jill's lips as she heard this. But Mrs Trevennor noticed nothing. In her great relief she had forgotten the feud between the two children, and presently she kissed them both, and tucked

them in, and went downstairs. Paul had taken
his brother off to bed, and Margaret and the
rector were alone in the dining-room. Both
turned as she came in.

'Meg, come and sit down; you look worn-
out,' said the rector, pulling an easy-chair up
to the fire.—'Peggy, run and get your mother
some coffee, dear. Oh yes, and boil her an
egg, and bring some bread and butter.'

'Yes, daddy,' replied Margaret.

'An egg! At nearly twelve o'clock at
night!' gasped his wife. 'Oh, Arthur, I
can't! I should love the coffee, but I can't
eat an egg!'

'Run along, Peg, and do as I told you,'
he said serenely.—'Meg, you are done-up!
You must have something!'

Mrs Trevennor argued no more. In truth
she was utterly worn-out. The anxiety she
had endured as the minutes passed slowly from
eight o'clock to half-past, from half-past eight
to nine o'clock, and onwards; the agony she
had felt when the messenger sent to the
Comptons' returned saying that Larry and
the girls had left the Manor before eight; the
horror of that moment when Larry had lost
consciousness, had taken much out of her.
She leaned back in her chair and closed her
eyes.

The rector looked at her anxiously, but said nothing. Presently she sat up.

'How stupid I am!' she said with an assumption of her usual brightness. 'Arthur, you must be as tired as I am. Here's Peggy with the coffee!—Peggy, darling, what a good girl you are to your old mother! You've only brought two cups; run and get a third. There's plenty for us all—oh, and Paul!'

'I'm going to take Paul's up to him,' explained Margaret. 'He said he would not leave Larry till he was asleep. He's changed beds with Bear, and he said I was to tell you not to worry, 'cos there's nothing wrong with the kid but nerves, and a good rest will put him right. I'm going to take the coffee up now, and I sha'n't come down again. You can leave the tray there, and I'll get it in the morning. Good-night!' She kissed her hand to them, and danced off, and presently they heard the jingling of china on the tray as she went upstairs.

They sat quietly together for a while; then the rector rose to his feet. 'I'm going to carry you up to bed, Meg.'

'Indeed you're not!' returned his wife. 'Listen! There's one! Come along, Arthur; we'll go the rounds and see that they're all safe.' Her voice ended with a little quaver. She was thinking how easily she might have been listening to heavy footfalls, the steps of men bearing something immovable, broken, lifeless. The rector felt the current of her thoughts.

'Thank God, dearest, it isn't so!' he said. 'Let's go and look at them to drive the bogies away.'

Upstairs everything was in order. In the night nursery the four younger ones slumbered peacefully; Margaret was sleeping with Gerry that night, and they found her fast asleep with the little girl in her arms. Jill and Nell were also in the land of dreams; Bear was snoring lustily in Paul's room; and in the big attic usually shared by the three middle boys Larry lay, a shade paler than usual, with purple shadows under his eyes, showing the awfulness of the strain he had undergone, but sleeping quietly, and safe.

Paul was the only one of the children awake, and he was sitting on the end of Bear's bed thoughtfully cleaning out his pipe. He looked up as his parents entered. 'Hello!' he said cheerfully. 'I kicked Bear out because I thought old Larry might be a bit restless! He looks all right, though, doesn't he?'

His mother bent and kissed him. 'Good-night,' she said. 'You are a comfort to me, Paul—you and Peggy.'

'You and Peggy, good children both!' added the rector.

Paul reddened beneath the praise. 'Oh, that's all right!' he said. ''Night! Make the mater stay in bed to-morrow, pater, eh?'

His father nodded smilingly. 'I shall play tyrant, Paul! Good-night, old man!'

''Night, dad!'

An hour later there was darkness all over the house, and peace had once more descended on it.

CHAPTER XIII.

'IT was my own fault, you know,' said Larry suddenly.

It was Sunday afternoon. The rector, Paul, and Helen had gone to Sunday School as usual; Mrs Trevennor was in bed, where her husband had insisted on her spending the day; and Jill was in her room, with Sheila for company. Cecil, who was much better, was up in the nursery with Gerry and the babies, and Margaret had felt free to devote herself to her brother.

He was lying on the couch in the drawing-room, looking very white, with heavy shadows under his eyes. The reaction had set in, and any movement brought about violent pains in his head. Paul and the rector had brought him downstairs between them after the midday dinner, and he was settled for the rest of the day. He had been lying so still that Margaret, sitting reading by the window, had thought him asleep until his speech startled her. She got up and crossed the room to him, curling up on the rug, and laying her head against the couch. 'What was your own fault, Larry?' she said.

'Last night's affair. If we had been killed or hurt, I should have been to blame!'

'Nonsense, dear!' returned his sister. 'Firefly is very high-spirited, and Nell said it was Jem Gough made her shy.'

'That's true enough. But I forgot what the pater said about seeing that she had no oats. They gave her a good feed, and she was fresh to start with. If anything had happened to Nell and Gerry, it would have been my fault entirely—no one else's!'

'Well, if you hadn't kept your head as you did, you would all have been killed,' returned his sister. 'Don't think it again, old man!'

Larry moved restlessly on the couch. 'It's all very well talking!' he replied impatiently. 'But can't you see, Peggy, it was my criminal neglect that caused the whole thing? And how do we know that it hasn't hurt that kid Gerry? She's a nervy little thing; she's had a quiet life—a dashed quiet life! What's all this upset going to do to her? Peg, I wish you'd fetch her. I want to see for myself that there's nothing wrong, and I haven't seen her all day. It's different for Nell, you know. She's steadier altogether; and she's accustomed to sudden shocks. But Gerry isn't. Do fetch her, old girl!'

Margaret got up instantly. She realised that Larry was in a very highly strung condition, and that it might be some little time before his nerve came back to him. He had had an awful shock, and she felt that he must be kept quiet. It rather startled her to see the calm, self-contained Larry in this condition. She ran upstairs to the nursery, and found Gerry sitting playing at 'Consequences' with Cecil. 'Gerry, will you come downstairs?' she asked. 'Larry wants you!'

Gerry nodded, and got up at once. 'All right, Peggy; I'm coming.'

She clung nervously to Margaret's hand as they went downstairs. It would be a long time before she got over the shock of last night's adventure. Margaret, glancing down at her, saw that she was as white as the pinafore she was wearing, and that her eyes looked larger than ever. 'You're all right, kiddie, aren't you?' she said.

'Yes, I'm all right. Is Larry here?'

She went into the drawing-room, and up to the couch.

Larry held out his hand to her. 'Come here, you little beggar! Let's have a look at you.' He inspected her closely, till the ready colour rose to her cheeks. 'You're all right, eh?'

'Yes, thank you, Larry. Nell says you saved our lives! I wanted to thank you for it. It was so good of you!'

Larry roared at that. 'Oh, you kid, you'll kill me! Why, you little ass, it wasn't good of me at all. Common-sense!'

Gerry looked at him, the glimmering of a smile in her eyes. 'Oh yes; I see. It was stupid to say that, wasn't it?'

'Very!' he chuckled. 'Curl up on the rug there beside Peg.'

'Nothing doing!' returned the latter young lady decidedly. 'I'm going to see about tea! —Keep an eye on him, Gerry, will you? Dad and the others will be in presently, and I must get tea ready now.'

'Oh, come off it,' remarked the invalid. 'Keep an eye on him? I'll have to keep an eye on her, you mean!'

'Oh, keep an eye on each other, then!' laughed his sister. She went out, closing the door quietly behind her, and ran upstairs to see her mother with a light heart.

'They're all right now, mums,' she said as she sat down. 'Gerry thanked Larry for saving her life! Said it was "so good of him." I wish you'd seen his face! They're playing nursemaid to each other now, and I'm going to get tea. Do you want anything while I'm here?'

'Nothing, thank you, dear,' replied Mrs Trevennor, who had been paying the price of last night's anxiety by a headache, and was feeling weary and washed-out. 'I think I will get to sleep now that I know they are both all right. Oh, Peggy, Peggy, when I think of the terrible news I might have had to send to Madeira and I haven't, I feel I can't thank God enough!'

'It would have been dreadful for us all,' murmured Margaret, as she deftly turned her mother's pillow. 'Try to sleep now, darling, and I'll bring you some tea later.'

Down in the drawing-room Gerry was sitting telling Larry all about her life at Dumberley, and entertaining that youth vastly.

'And you never heard of hockey or lacrosse until you came here?' he said incredulously.

'No! You see, Aunt Charlotte and Aunt Alicia were too old to play games much, and there was no one else,' replied Gerry wistfully.

'What awful rot!' returned Larry sympathetically. 'You must have had a thin time of it!'

At this juncture the rector came in. He glanced keenly at the pair, but what he saw reassured him. Both looked more like themselves than they had done all day, and he felt very thankful. After a laughing word or two he went upstairs to his wife, leaving the young ones together.

Margaret, aided by Nell, took their tea upstairs, and sent some up to Jill and Sheila. Then she wrapped Cecil up, and brought him and the babies down to the drawing-room, where Bernard, seated on the coal-box, with his father's glasses perched on his impertinent nose, and a copy of *Soldiers Three* in his hands, was giving a life-like imitation of his mathematical master's endeavour to teach him something.

'Now, Trevennor! Sit up, sir! If $x^2 + y + 3y^3 = 676x^2 + xy + y^2$—— Trevennor, close that book! How often am I to tell you I will not permit fidgeting?'

At this point the instructor's glasses fell off, and in his efforts to catch them he nearly upset the cake-stand. His sisters fell on him with shrieks of dismay, and he was banished to the other side of the fireplace, with the threat hanging over him of being sent to the kitchen for his tea if he did not behave himself.

'That's the worst of *girls*!' mumbled the aggrieved youth as he betook himself to his new seat. 'You try to amuse 'em, an' then, if there's a spill or anythin', they shriek at you an' stop your fun! I'm fed-up!'

'Then you won't want any tea!' retorted Helen smartly.

'Oh, won't I? That's where you make the mistake, young woman! I do!'

'Well, hand the cups round, then, and do something for your living,' suggested Margaret.—'Geoff and Betty, here is your milk. Don't make too much mess on the rug!'

'Whose maths. set are you in?' inquired Paul, when at length they were all settled.

'Lorrimer's. He's a good sort, really, you know. Why?'

'Poor beggar! So that's why he looks so mournful always. I've often wondered,' grinned Larry.

'Oh no, that isn't it!' cried Gerry from her point of vantage beside Paul. 'It isn't that at all!'

'What is it, then?' demanded Cecil. 'An' what the dickens do you know about our beaks?'

'Well, I heard Lillie Tomson say to Betty Oliver that Mr Lorrimer was in love with Miss Hamilton,' explained Gerry, 'but Miss Hamilton wouldn't have anything to do with him.'

'Why not?'

'Lorrimer in love? What rot!'

'Curb your tongue, little pal!'

'Gerry, darling, I don't think you ought to say such things.'

Gerry turned her eyes on the last speaker, who was Margaret. 'Why not?' she said wonderingly. 'I think it's true.'

'You kids chatter a lot too much,' said Nell, with the robe of the prefect heavy upon her. 'Lillie Tomson is an awful little ass, and Betty Oliver isn't much better. Keep clear of them!'

Gerry turned to her pal and stand-by, Paul. 'Tell me, Paul,' she begged.

'Not cricket! Your Miss Hamilton wouldn't like it! Don't do it, little pal.'

Geoff got to his feet. He came over to Gerry, and stared at her with unwinking eyes. 'You and Paul pals?' he asked.

'Rather!' said Paul.

'Then I won't come wif you for walks any more.'

'Why not? What's that got to do with it?'

''Cos if I'm tired you won't cawwy me; you'll cawwy Gewwy.'

'Not if I know it!' laughed Paul. 'It's bad enough hauling you about, but Gerry would be the pink limit!'

''Sides, I don't like being carried,' added Gerry with dignity.

At this point an animated hockey discussion among the other members of the company broke up, since Margaret questioned loudly as to where the sugar-basin had got to. 'Where is it?' she demanded. 'It was here ten minutes ago!—Cecil, have you taken it?'

''Course I haven't, silly!'

'Bear, then?—Geoff?—Gerry, you wouldn't?'

'She hasn't stirred since we began tea, anyhow,' said Paul. 'Where's baby gone to?'

They looked round. When last she had been noticed, Betty had been sitting curled up on the hearthrug placidly munching a sugary bun. Now she had vanished as completely as the sugar-basin. A yell from Bernard announced her discovery behind a screen. He brought her forth, and she trotted gaily along, holding up the empty sugar-basin, and demanding with sweet, limpid eyes 'More sudar, Peddy!'

'What a nuisance!—Baby, you ought to be spanked!—Gerry dear, just run down to the kitchen and ask Mary for some more sugar, will you?'

Gerry rose to her feet, a feeling of horror filling her. She was naturally afraid of the dark, and the passage which led to the kitchen was specially dusky. She opened her lips to say so, but caught Cecil's eye, and thought better of it. She had shown herself a coward the night before. She couldn't do that again. So she took the basin and set off on her errand.

How dark it was in the passage! She had to go past the stairs, and who knew what awful thing might not be lying in wait for her, concealed half-way up? Supposing a long, skinny hand came through the railings and clutched her hair! But she got safely past without anything happening, and reached the kitchen door, which Mary, attracted by foot-steps, had opened. 'Come in, Miss Gerry!' she said heartily. 'What is it now? Sugar? Very well! Just a minute!'

How Gerry wished that it might be longer than a minute! But no. Mary filled the basin and returned it to her, and she had to set off on her fearsome journey back to the drawing-room. A moment later the entire family was startled by a scream which rang through the house, and then Gerry burst into the drawing-room, tripped over a footstool, and lay where she was, sobbing affrightedly, while the sugar lay all over the floor.

Margaret and Paul both sprang to her; but Paul was there first, and it was in his arms that she sobbed out something about 'a horrid wild animal or a ghost which snatched at her feet as she passed.' Bernard promptly seized the matches and tore out into the passage, followed by Nell and Geoff. They came back in a minute, bearing the author of the mischief with them.

'Miss Brown!' cried Larry. 'She's been up to her old tricks again! Oh, Miss Brown!'

Miss Brown, a ginger cat of wild and rakish demeanour, struggled violently in Bernard's arms till he put her down, when she stalked across the room to the window and mewed to be let out.

'Look, Gerry,' said Margaret, as she hastened to comply with the request, 'it's only Miss Brown. Don't cry, dear.'

Gerry made an effort to choke down her tears, and presently succeeded. But she was still so nervous that Paul declined to go to church that night, and sat with her and the little ones and Larry, reading to them from the old d'Aulnoy fairy-book till bed-time.

After she was in bed Nell came and sat beside her till she fell asleep, and twice during the night Paul crept down to see that she was all right.

His mother had once said of her eldest

born, 'There is a good deal of the woman in Paul as well as the man,' and it was true. Gerry had appealed to his protective instincts in a way that his hardier brothers and sisters failed to do, and, having assumed the care of her, he was determined to leave undone nothing which could help her. Larry was awake when Paul returned the second time, and he looked at him curiously. 'You're a good sort, old bean!' he remarked.

'Oh, shut up!' grunted Paul. 'I'm going back to my own room to-morrow, an' you can have the champion snorer back!'

CHAPTER XIV.

THE FAGS DECIDE TO STRIKE.

FORMS III.A and III.B were in a ferment. That day it had seemed good to Marcia and her peers to issue an edict, saying that all girls below Form A must report to the prefects' room each morning by a quarter to nine to show that they had changed their shoes, and as long as the bad weather lasted this must continue. The primary cause for this command lay in Miss Catcheside's having complained to her head girl that it seemed impossible to get the girls of the Lower School to change.

'The kindergarten do,' she had said. 'Miss Mitchell and Miss Rose see to that. But from I. to IV.B one would think slippers had never been invented. It's really dreadful, Marcia!'

'It is,' agreed Marcia. 'I'll see what I can do, Miss Catcheside.'

The Head smiled at her in the way which always inspired the school captain with the same feelings as she inspired in a large number of the younger girls. 'Thank you, Marcia; 1 should be so glad if you would. The staff really have so much to do, I don't like adding to their responsibilities.'

Marcia had then discussed the matter with her colleagues, and the result had been the new order which was causing such a disturbance.

'Go and report to the prefects!' gasped Olive Purvis. 'Whatever next, I should like to know?'

'The next thing, my dear, will be that the prefects come and wash our faces for us,' retorted Leo Fairless.

'Simply idiotic, I call it!' fumed Kitty O'Connell. 'Marcia is getting a bit above herself; don't you think so, Gerry?'

But for once Gerry Challoner had no answer ready.

It was now a month since that afternoon in the cinema when Marcia had first awakened intense adoration in that impressionable little heart of hers, and the adoration had not abated in the least. In that month Gerry had learned a good deal that was not included in the school curriculum. She had learned that, while one may grouse in school about existing conditions, out of school one proclaims its superiority to all others; that juniors may vow vengeance for wrongs done by the seniors, but that if the seniors come along and exert any authority, that authority is rarely, if ever, defied; that truth must be spoken on all occasions unless it means getting some one else into trouble, but that in that case if it is impossible to keep silent, then you must lie with conviction.

Life at the Rectory had further taught her to talk slang, to whistle, to slide down the banisters, climb trees, slam doors, tear her clothes, and stand teasing. When the Misses Challenor returned from Madeira, it is to be feared that they would scarcely approve of the change in their great-niece; but the Trevennors, with one exception, hailed it with delight. As Bernard said, it had always been there, but it was they who had brought it out.

Among her classmates Gerry was soon recognised as a person of character and decision. In form, her chums were Con and Muriel; out of form, she had Gwen Compton, Tessa Donati, and, in a lesser degree, Rosamund and Francesca Atherton. But these two people were very popular, and both were two forms ahead of her, so that she did not see much of them. At school she was very happy. She enjoyed most of her lessons, and

was beginning to make rapid strides. For
music she had Tessa's father, Signor Donati.
He was a little, nervous man, intensely musical, and dreadfully short-tempered; but he
possessed a genius for teaching, and under
him Gerry progressed as she had never done
before. He took a great liking for the little
girl, whose liquid dark eyes shone so, and
grew so big with ecstasy when, sitting down
at the piano, he drew from it such wonderful
harmonies that on more than one occasion
she cried for sheer delight.

But to return to the new order and Kitty
O'Connell. After waiting for Gerry's answer
for a moment or two, she shook the young
lady impatiently. 'Gerry Challoner, wake
up!' she cried. 'I'm going to have a meeting of the Lower School now!—Come on,
every one!'

They poured after her into the gymnasium,
which happened to be empty just then.
Kitty mounted on to the vaulting-horse,
while the others grouped round her, and a
meeting was held.

'It's a shame!' began Kitty. 'We might
just as well be babies! And it's just inter-
feringness! They don't really care if we do
change our shoes or not; it's just so they
can boss us round more than they do now,

and I say it's a horrid shame! Look at what they've done this term! We mayn't even whisper between the lessons; we mayn't walk any more than three together when we leave school; we've to talk French in the cloakroom; and now, this! It's the limit, and I vote we don't stand it any longer!'

Here a particularly emphatic gesture sent her plunging off her perch into Con's out-stretched arms, and her speech came to a premature end. However, Olive Purvis, Muriel Hatherley, Sybil Forsyth, and Betty Oliver all took her place in turns, and de-livered themselves of heated, if somewhat ungrammatical, orations, which were wildly applauded. Just as Con climbed up, how-ever, to give the audience her views on the subject the two-twenty-five bell rang, and the meeting had perforce to break up and dis-perse to its form rooms. It was a mercy for all of them that it was one of the 'full prep.' afternoons, for every one was far too aggrieved to have paid any attention to lessons. As it was, Miss Hamilton and Miss Hildreth, who had charge of Forms IV.A and IV.B, III.A and III.B, were obliged to distribute sundry order marks, and every single member of the secret society bore home, in addition to her other work, thirty lines of poetry to be repeated perfectly on the morrow.

'It's a shame!' grumbled Gwen to Gerry as they walked to the station. 'Thirty lines of "The Armada." Hammy's a pig!'

'Well, it's worse for Kitty and Leo and Tessa,' replied Gerry philosophically. 'I don't mind "The Armada" so much; it rhymes! But they have that silly speech of Phebe's in *As You Like It* about Rosalind, and Shakespeare never rhymes!'

'Hammy ought to be ashamed of herself!' agreed Gwen. Then she collided with some one, and looked up to find that it was the mistress of whom she had just spoken, which so overcame her that she could find nothing to say.

Miss Hamilton, obviously in a hurry, merely glanced at her pupils, and with a 'Good-bye, girls!' hurried on, leaving them still speechless. This state of affairs lasted till they reached the station, to find the train in, and Marcia and Nell waiting for them in anything but a good temper.

'Hurry up, you little snails!' flashed Marcia. 'Where on earth have you been all this time?'

'We've come as quickly as we could,' returned Gwen.

'It looks like it! Go and sit down! Another time you'll set off before we do! Now, hurry up, and don't stand all over the carriage!'

'Don't intend to!—Come on, Gerry; we'll leave their high and mightinesses, and find another compartment!'

Gwen tugged Gerry by the sleeve, and the two younger girls slipped away, leaving the outraged prefects to gasp at their audacity.

'It's all very well in school,' groused Gwen to a select audience of the Athertons, Muriel Hatherley, Lillie Tomson, Gerry, and Mary Anderson, 'but I'm not going to be prefected out of school!'

'Not going to be what?' demanded Con.

'Oh, bossed round by Marcia! That's the worst of sisters!'

'Gerry Challoner, you've to come to the captain's carriage,' observed Madeleine's voice at this juncture.

'Don't go!' urged Gwen. 'This isn't school! She hasn't any right to order you about!'

Such open defiance almost bereft Madeleine of speech. However, she gave Gerry no option of going or staying, for, laying a firm hand on the small shoulder, she drew her away, leaving her juniors furious.

'It's about time we did something!' said Con when at last they could talk coherently. 'These seniors jolly well want sitting on!'

'We ought to strike,' replied Muriel. 'I'm going to!'

'So'm I! We all ought to, an' I vote we do!'

'How do we start?' asked Allegra Atherton.

'Oh—er—well, we tell them we won't do as they tell us.'

'An' who's going to do the telling?' demanded Rosamund. 'It doesn't affect me, 'cos I'm not fagged now; but I'd like to see any of you telling Marcia you wouldn't do as she told you!'

'We sha'n't tell her, silly! We'll write it, of course!'

'Well, if you're going to strike—but I think it's perfectly idiotic—I advise you to get every one else to.'

'Of course we will! We aren't quite idiots! An' now I'm going to get some of that beastly "Armada" learnt. Hammy's a cat!' And Gwen resolutely opened her *Lays of Ancient Rome* and buried herself in it.

The net result of all this was that a meeting of the Lower School was called in the gym. after dinner next day, when various leading members of it pointed out, with more or less disregard for the rules of English grammar, that Britons never, never would be slaves, and that the Sixth were exceeding their privileges, and needed taking down a peg or two. Grievances of two terms before were raked up, and the whole party became very much excited and inflamed, and it was finally decided that there should be no more fagging.

'How are we going to let them know?' asked Leo. 'Do we just begin to-morrow by doing nothing?'

'Well, we can't go round telling them we're not going to do as we're told, can we?' said Myfanwy.

'We'll write it,' replied Kitty, who, as usual, took the lead. 'We'll make it up and sign it, and then Gerry Challenor shall write it out—Hammy says she's the best writer in the Lower School—and I'll come to school early to-morrow morning and put it on the table. Who's got any paper and envelopes?'

'I have,' volunteered Tessa.

'Oh, good! We'll do it now, then!'

'I can copy it during prep.,' added Gerry, 'and we can pass it round to be signed. It's Mademoiselle's prep. with us to-day.'

'All right for you,' replied Leo; 'but how are we going to get hold of it?'

'I'll ask to come and borrow Rose's French dicker,' suggested Con; 'then I can give it to her, and she can pass it to Tess.'

As the two Fourths did preparation together, this seemed an excellent way of solving the difficulty, and it was agreed that Tessa should make some errand to the Second Form room later on, and leave the notice in Sybil Forsyth's keeping. The First Form were not fagged, so, as Muriel remarked, it didn't matter about them.

'But you must promise on your word of honour not to tell any one,' she concluded.

''Course not! We aren't sneaks!' retorted Betty Oliver, bristling up.

'Oh, I don't think you would on purpose,' explained Muriel; 'but it's so easy to let something slip!'

'Well, we won't! You needn't worry!'

It is to be feared that very little preparation was done in either the Lower or the Lower Middle School that afternoon. The strike warning was composed, and handed to Gerry by Kitty during the needlework hour. Gerry copied it out, and it went the round of III.A and III.B. Rosamund Atherton, though not a fag, was far too fond of mischief to spoil sport, and when Con had left the room she neatly passed on the note to Tessa, and later it was smuggled out of the Fourth Form room into the Second, and at four o'clock was delivered to Kitty by Betty.

Kitty took it with a chuckle. 'What a shock they'll get to-morrow!' she said.

CHAPTER XV.

THE STRIKE.

NOTHING recking of what awaited her on the table in the prefects' room, Marcia sat chatting to Nell in the train. 'Gerry is coming on at hockey,' she said presently. 'How nervous the child is, though! Did you notice how she coloured when I told her so on Monday?'

'In the train, you mean?' asked Madeleine, looking up from her history for a moment. 'I thought she was going to cry; didn't you?'

'Overcome by the honour!' laughed Claire. 'Shall you promote her to the Sixth Eleven, Nell? I almost think she's worth it.'

'I don't know,' returned Nell. 'There are only two places, you see, and Olive Purvis must have one of them. That leaves one place, and there are Betty Oliver and Allegra Atherton to be taken into account.'

'By the way,' said Madeleine, closing her book and laying it down, 'have you noticed anything in these forms—anything about the way they're behaving, I mean?'

'Nothing special,' replied Nell. 'Why? Have you?'

'They're a cheeky set,' observed Claire thoughtfully; 'but I don't think there's anything much the matter with them beyond that. What do you say, Marcia?'

Marcia raised troubled eyes to the speaker's face. 'I know what Maddie means,' she said slowly. 'It isn't absolute defiance, but—well, I can't express it.'

'I shouldn't be at all surprised if there was an explosion,' said Madeleine, 'especially with the Fifth. You know Alicia isn't very tactful, and she orders them about, and I know she's got their backs up!'

'The trouble began with that little idiot Mary Anderson,' returned Marcia. 'She never remembers anything; and when she was hockey fag, she gave the Second a bad time of it with her carelessness. I suppose Alicia has really been trying to guard against that sort of thing again.'

'Very probably,' replied Madeleine dryly. 'And she's making them hate her!'

'Well, it won't do very much harm, really!' interrupted Claire.

'My dear girl, it will do all the harm in the world—it will lower the tone of the whole school! "In union is strength," you know.'

'Well, how are you going to settle it, then?'

'I don't know! I only wish I did!'

'Things may settle themselves,' put in Nell; 'and here we are!'

In the prefects' room they found Philippa Southern and Hazel Burnham, two Dawley girls, who happened to be respectively the school librarian and editress of the magazine. They both greeted the four with animation, and a demand to know whether or not requests should be made with regard to subscriptions for a new bookcase.

'We really are getting crowded out,' said Philippa, a tall, graceful girl of seventeen. 'Hazel thought you might put an appeal in the mag., Marcia. What do you think?'

The discussion which followed lasted till the entrance of the youngest prefect, who was also the school beauty—a dark-haired, dark-eyed girl of sixteen, cousin of Tessa Donati, and named Concetta Donati. She held out a large square envelope to the captain. 'Some admirer has been writing to you, Marcia,' she laughed. 'What a thickness it is!'

'"Urgent,"' read Elsie Meredith over Marcia's shoulder. 'Goodness, Marcia, what can those children have to say that is urgent?'

'Haven't the foggiest notion,' replied Marcia, as she slit open the envelope. 'Why, it's a list of names!'

'Must be some petition,' said Nell.

'Something against fagging!' laughed Claire. 'Why—Marcia——'

Marcia stood reading the message over and over. She had gone perfectly white, and her eyes gleamed with a cold, steely light. Then she turned to the others. 'Listen to this!' she said tensely. 'I never heard of such impertinence in my life!' And in a clear voice she read the following effusion:

'"DEAR MARCIA,—This is to say that as none of the Upper School can treat us decently, we are not going to fag for you any more. We are on strike. If you wish to negotiate with us, any communications may be addressed to our leaders, Kathleen O'Connell, Gwenna Compton, or Tessa Donati.—Yours affectionately."'

Here followed a long string of names, which Marcia did not trouble to read aloud. There was a deathly silence in the room.

Claire broke it. 'Who has written it, Marcia?'

'The handwriting is Gerry Challoner's,' returned Marcia, with thin lips.

'Gerry Challoner! That mouse!' ejaculated Philippa Southern.

'Gerry never composed that!' declared Nell.

'I don't think she did,' replied Marcia. 'It is considerably more like Kitty O'Connell than any one else in those forms.'

'Well, what are we going to do?' asked Elsie Meredith.

'Take no notice of it or them for the present,' replied Marcia. 'Instead of prep. from twelve to one we'll hold a prefects' meeting, but don't let any one outside of ourselves know. I wouldn't give those imps that satisfaction for worlds. She glanced round her colleagues rapidly. 'Judith Fitzgerald and Jessie Mackay aren't here.— Concetta, aren't they in your form?'

'Yes,' said Concetta.

'Then you might warn them, will you? And meanwhile don't let any one outside of ourselves know.'

'What about the rest of VI.B?' objected Hazel Burnham. 'They're safe to wonder why we leave the room instead of "prep-ing" with them as usual.'

'Who are there?'

Hazel made a hasty reconnoitre in her memory. 'Edith Oliver, Hester Brown, Florence Anderson, and the two Bakers.'

'And Muriel Purvis and Letty Harrison,' supplemented Olwen Tudor.

Marcia turned to a tall, serious girl who had not yet spoken. 'Pauline, what do you advise? Whatever we do, we mustn't let the Lower School think we're upset in any way.'

Pauline nodded. 'I quite agree with you there, Marcia; but beyond taking them into our confidence and asking them to say nothing, I don't see what we can do.'

'Yes, and I can hear Hester Brown and Letty Harrison saying nothing!' said Nell. 'I believe those two will talk in their graves.'

'Oh, Nell, if we put them on their honour!'

'Oh, they wouldn't mean to,' agreed Nell; 'but they just couldn't help it!'

'And what are you going to do about the Fifth?' asked somebody.

This question was concluded by a knock on the door, and in response to Marcia's curt 'Come in!' Alicia Brett, captain of the Second Hockey Eleven and leader of Form V.A, burst in, looking flushed and angry. She was accompanied by Rosemary Drewe, who was generally spokesman for V.B. Both held letters in their hands, and both were excited. Marcia guessed at once what they had come

about, but she merely said, 'Good-morning!
Do you want me?'

'Marcia, read that!' choked Alicia. 'Such
cheek!'

Marcia took the note and skimmed it
through. It was a copy, in Kitty O'Connell's
big, untidy writing, of the letter she had received, the only difference being that in this
case it was signed by the three 'leaders.'
Rosemary's proved to be the same.

'I suppose you don't want these?' asked
the captain when she had finished them.

Rosemary, a small girl of fifteen, with a
humorous mouth, laughed. 'Well, scarcely!
What shall we do about it, Marcia?'

'Nothing at present,' replied Marcia.
'Don't take any notice of either it or them.
—And, Alicia, don't let them know you are
annoyed.'

It seemed a necessary warning, for, as Concetta afterwards said, Alicia looked ready to
choke with fury. The prayer-bell rang just
then, and the two Fifth Formers withdrew,
leaving the prefects gazing at each other in
a troubled silence.

'It's largely Alicia's fault,' said Nell at
length. 'She has ragged those kids dreadfully, you know. She can't keep her temper!'

'I know,' replied Marcia curtly. 'But, all

the same, they've a good cheek to attempt this!—Come to prayers now, you people. I shall think this over, and we'll call a meeting, as I said, at twelve o'clock.—Here, Hazel, just put this rubbish in your case for the present, will you? We'd better keep it till we've settled with them, I suppose.' And she tossed the three 'notices' over to Hazel, who fielded them neatly, and locked them up in her attaché-case.

Then the grandees of the school went to prayers, though in anything but a prayerful mood. Indeed, through the morning they could think of nothing else but the extraordinary action taken by the juniors, and the staff concerned with them began to wonder whatever had happened to them. They kept to Marcia's command to say nothing to the juniors, and those people might never have existed for the amount of notice they took of them.

This state of things first piqued, then alarmed, those young persons. 'I don't think they can have got the notes,' said Lillie Tomson at break when the secret society clustered together in a corner of the playground. 'Did you send the Fifth Form ones, Kitty?'

'Oh, they've *got* them all right,' returned Kitty. 'I wonder what they mean to do!'

But that was a mystery no one could elucidate at present, and they had to return to lessons with their curiosity still unsatisfied. But at twelve o'clock Tessa Donati, returning from her piano-lesson, saw Judith Fitzgerald and Olwen Tudor going into the prefects' room. She passed on this news to Con Atherton, whom she met farther down the corridor, and contrived to pass a note about it round her own form.

'Prefects' meeting!' murmured those ladies mentally. 'What will happen?'

CHAPTER XVI.

THE PREFECTS' MEETING.

IN the prefects' room the sixteen people who were more or less responsible for the government of the school were seating themselves round the table with due regard for precedence and school etiquette. At the head of the table sat Marcia, looking very stern and judicial; on her right hand was Pauline Norton, who was second prefect, and on the other Elsie Meredith, third prefect; Helen Trevennor and Claire Ashe, as hockey and cricket captains respectively, came next; then Philippa and Hazel. Swimming and tennis, in the persons of Pamela Hethcote and Dorothy Young, were next; and Eileen Kearney and Doris Weatherby represented art and music. The Lower Sixth prefects— Concetta Donati, Olwen Tudor, Judith Fitzgerald, and Jessie Mackay—sat at the foot of the table. Each girl had paper and pencil in front of her, and all looked intensely serious. Marcia called the roll, and then, rising to her feet, briefly recounted the reason for their meeting. 'I think,' she concluded, 'that you will all agree with me that this is a very serious matter. Practically the entire Lower School has risen in rebellion against the Upper School. We cannot, for one moment, permit this state of things to go on. At the same time, neither can we involve the staff in the affair. We must settle it ourselves, and settle it at once. I shall be glad of any sug- gestions you may have to make which will enable us to cope with it.' She sat down amid faint applause, which she instantly crushed with a frown, and there was silence for a few minutes.

Then Pamela rose to her feet. 'Marcia,' she said, 'may we see the note they sent you?'

'Certainly,' replied Marcia. 'Hazel, you have it, I believe.'

Hazel produced it from her case, and it was passed round.

'The entire school from IV.B to II.,' com- mented Judith. 'That makes things rather difficult, doesn't it?'

'It certainly doesn't make them any easier,' replied Marcia.

There was silence again, broken by Pauline rising to her feet. 'I hope you won't think I'm going against our Order,' she began, 'but it seems to me that it's only fair to find out definitely why they are striking.'

Marcia raised her head sharply. 'They've given us the reason,' she said.

'Only that "none of the seniors treat us decently,"' quoted Pauline, with a glance at the paper. 'It's too vague, Marcia; we must tie them to facts.'

'I agree,' said Madeleine, rising also. 'Of course, we can all guess what's begun it— Alicia Brett. But they must have some other reason besides that. Kitty O'Connell is a mad Irishwoman—saving your presences!' she added with a laughing glance at Eileen and Judith. 'But Tessa and Gerry and Dorothy Cornwall and some of those others are level-headed enough.'

'More than I can say for Gwen!' said Marcia tersely, glancing at the list as she spoke. 'I see Gloria is in it, Judith; Daphne Hethcote and Molly Kearney, too!'

'To say nothing of Rosalie,' added Philippa; 'and is that Althea's name at the bottom there? Yes, it is! Well, my family appear to be up to the neck in it!'

'Oh, the Second only signed because they saw the others do it,' said Nell hastily. 'If you come to that, Gerry and Sheila are both in it too.'

'I don't see what it matters,' said Pauline. 'We can't say anything at home. That wouldn't be fair at all!'

'Well, what are we going to do?' demanded Claire impatiently.

'I propose we ask them to send their delegates—isn't that the word?—and find out what is really at the bottom of it,' laughed Judith. 'After all, it's only what the great owners of mills and mines and railways have to do.'

'It won't be letting the Sixth down, will it?' queried Olwen anxiously.

They all looked at Marcia for an answer to this. 'No,' she said slowly. 'As Pauline says, we must be fair. We can't condemn them unheard, so I suppose we must just listen to what they have to say. But it's very annoying; and if Alicia really is at the bottom of it, I shall feel like wringing her neck!'

'I wonder who they'll send?' said Dorothy, as she idly scribbled on her paper.

'Kitty O'Connell for a certainty,' replied Nell; 'Con Atherton and Tessa Donati, of course. The Second will send Betty Oliver, and III.B will send Allegra Atherton. Funny how those Atherton children lead in all their forms!'

'They're a remarkably clever family,' said Marcia absently. 'Well, are we all agreed— we send for their delegates, and hear what they have to say?'

'It certainly seems the best thing to do under the circumstances.'

'Oh, rather, Marcia!'

'Might as well! But it's a nuisance!'

'Can you suggest anything better, then, Doris? Something must be done!'

Doris Weatherby shook her head. She was infinitely cleverer at harmony than organisation; her pianoforte work was vastly superior to her school government. Indeed, as Marcia once said, it was rather a pity she hadn't stayed in the Lower Sixth, because then she need not have been a prefect, and, in any case, Concetta Donati, who was merely vice-president of the Musical, really ran that club.

'Well,' said Nell briskly, 'it's nearly twenty to one, you people. I vote we concoct an epistle to their precious leaders, and invite their dele—what-d'you-call-'ems—to come here at two sharp. What do you say?'

'It seems to be the only thing to do,' agreed Marcia slowly.—'Give me some writing-paper, please, some one.'

Hazel provided her with some, and Elsie proffered her fountain-pen.

'Just make it plain and to the point, I suppose?' she queried.

'I should think so,' agreed Pamela; 'and in the third person.'

'Yes; we don't want any more fiascos of "yours affectionately" after a smashing shock of any kind,' laughed Claire, who was rarely known to take things seriously.

'It is scarcely likely I should make such a *faux pas* as that,' replied Marcia coldly.

'What a squash! Shall I get under the table? Don't be cross, Marcia! I was only joking;' and Claire smiled sunnily.

'This isn't a joking matter! Seriously, Claire, you mustn't try to turn it into one. We don't want those imps to imagine they've done anything clever.' But Marcia's face had lightened. It was difficult to resist Claire.

'Well, what are you going to say?' asked Dorothy.

'"The prefects beg to inform the Junior School that they will be in the prefects' room at two o'clock this afternoon, and are willing to receive their delegates then." How will that do?' asked Hazel.

'Splendidly! Couldn't be better! It's dignified, and yet not too crushing!'

'Well done you, Hazel!'

'Good! When I'm a wealthy woman with

piles of correspondence to attend to, I'll engage you as my secretary! I sha'n't forget!' This last was Claire, of course.

'I sha'n't either! But I shall require a jolly big screw.'

The meeting was taking a lighter turn. The feeling of tension had relaxed, and every one was willing to turn her attention to fun. Marcia wrote the note in her firm, pretty writing, enclosed it in an envelope, and addressed it to the Misses O'Connell, Compton, and Donati.

'How shall we get it to them?' she inquired as she finished.

Her question was answered by a knock at the door, when, in response to her 'Come in!' there entered Josie Atherton of the First Form, with a note from Miss Catcheside to say that, as the weather was so bad—it was sleeting—no one was to go outside after dinner, and would Marcia please see to it?

'It's all right,' said the school captain. Then she held up the note. 'Look here, child, can you give this to Kitty O'Connell at one o'clock?'

'Oh yes, Marcia!' returned Josie, very proud at being asked to do a service for the captain. 'Shall I put it in my blouse?'

'Yes. Take care of it,' said Marcia, as she

gave the precious missive to the little girl.
'Don't drop it round anywhere!'

'Oh, I won't! It will be quite safe!'

Marcia smiled as she pulled the child to her,
and dropped a hasty kiss on the black curls.
'There; run along now, kiddy!'

'And if you don't see Kitty,' added Pauline,
'Gwen Compton or Tessa Donati will do;
won't they, Marcia?' and she turned to the
captain.

'Yes,' replied Marcia; 'any one of those
three will do. Run along, Josie!'

Josie trotted obediently to the door. Arrived there, she suddenly turned. 'Oh,
Marcia, I do love you!' she breathed.
Then, overcome by what she had done, she
slipped out and raced down the corridor.

Nell turned with a smile to Marcia, who
had gone scarlet under this sudden tribute.
'I don't think it's you the kids object to,'
she smiled.

That great personage, the captain, went
redder than before. 'Oh, stop rotting!' she
said hurriedly.—'Now, you people, we've got
twenty minutes left. It's idiotic thinking of
trying to do any prep. Let's discuss the
concert. It's rather a good opportunity.'

They agreed that it was. St Peter's prided
itself on many things, and not the least of

them were its school concerts. They gave one at the end of each term, and they generally had good audiences. The Christmas concert was always the biggest affair. At Easter they usually gave a purely musical entertainment. Midsummer, being examination term, was characterised as a rule by a pageant, in which the senior girls, or, at any rate, those of them who were sitting for the public examinations, did as little as possible. But at Christmas they performed plays, and it was their boast that each succeeding one was better than its predecessors. On this occasion the Senior School was performing Laurence Housman's *Prunella*, and the Lower Middle and Lower Schools a dramatised version of *The Water-Babies*. The latter play was already in rehearsal, but the books for the former had just arrived, and it seemed good to Marcia to settle the parts, as far as possible, then. This interesting task occupied the time till the bell rang, and they decided to finish it after three o'clock that afternoon.

In the meantime Josie had found Kitty and given her the note. 'Marcia sends you this,' announced the messenger. 'I think it's very 'portant, 'cos she said to be careful.'

'Oh, trot along, baby!' said Kitty casually; 'and thanks awfully!'

Josie 'trotted along,' feeling highly indignant at being termed 'baby.'

The leader of the strikers retired to her form room, and summoned all such members of the secret society as were available.

'Come along! Marcia's written! Buck up, you folk! We've only two minutes.'

The note was slit open, and Marcia's message was read aloud. There was dead silence for a moment. Then Allegra Atherton broke it. 'What are "dellygates"?' she demanded.

'People who come from us to them to tell them what we want,' replied Kitty loftily. 'They always have them in strikes.'

'Well, who are we going to send? You three only?' queried Gloria Fitzgerald.

'That isn't fair!' protested Betty Oliver. 'Kitty an' Tessa are IV.B, and Gwen is III.A. But what about us? We ought to go too!'

By this time almost the entire Lower School, exclusive of the First Form and the Kindergarten, were assembled, so there was some point in Kitty's sarcastic, 'What! all of you? Better tell Marcia to see us in hall at that rate!'

'What are you children doing here?' demanded Miss Hamilton's voice at that moment.

'Do you know that the gong will sound in three minutes? Go to the Splasheries at once! —Kitty O'Connell, is this your doing?'

'Ye-yes!' stammered Kitty, turning very red.

'I thought so! After dinner you may come to me for some darning! I am surprised at you! Now go at once and wash your hands—at once, please!'

With Miss Hamilton looking like that it was of no use to protest, so the crestfallen leader had perforce meekly to go and wash her hands as she was told.

'I'm out of it,' she murmured to Gerry. 'You'll have to go instead of me.'

'Me!' gasped Gerry, regardless of grammar. 'But why me?'

''Cos you've got some sense!—Here, Annette,' she added to a small girl who was a member of III.B, and who possessed the further distinction of being Leo Fairless's sister, 'tell your people they are to choose two people to go to the prefects this afternoon. And pass it on to the Second!'

'All right, Kitty,' replied Annette. 'What time have we to be there?'

'Two o'clock,' grunted Kitty.—'We'll send two from each form,' she went on to Gerry. 'That ought to be sufficient, don't you think?'

'Oh, rather! Shall I tell them in III.A?' queried Gerry, as she retied her hair-ribbon.

'Yes; you might. Tell them you're going instead of me, and ask them to choose some one else as well, will you? So-long! I must see Gwen!' And Kitty rushed off at top-speed to communicate her ideas to Gwen and Tessa.

Gerry returned to her form room, and after considerable trouble got half of them to listen to her. 'We've got to choose some one to go to the prefects!' she yelled when finally she got silence. 'I've to go instead of Kitty, 'cos Hammy has nobbled her!'

Shades of Aunts Charlotte and Alicia! What they would have thought of their little great-niece had they seen her then, one shudders to think. Gerry was almost 'nobbled' herself. She scrambled down from her perch on Miss Hamilton's desk just before that lady herself entered the room, and retired to her own with all speed. The others hastily murmured together. Kathleen Raby, Mary Anderson, and Rachel Naylor were rather indignant at a new girl being chosen to represent them; but, on the whole, the form agreed that it was a good choice. Gerry was known to be what Con Atherton phrased as 'common-sensible,' and she could be trusted to keep her head. With regard to the other delegate there was no doubt at all. Con was almost unanimously chosen; and when, at dinner-time, they were settled down, Kitty contrived to convey to Gerry the news that from III.B Madge Hannay and Gertrude Trevena had been elected.

'Allegra Atherton a aller pour un musique-leçon,' she explained. 'Alors Madge et Gertrude venir avec vous.'

'Do you call that French, Kitty?' asked Miss Kennedy icily. 'Repeat your last sentence in English, please, and then I will give you the correct French.'

After dinner Kitty had to go to Miss Hamilton; but Gwen and Tessa, Gerry and Con, Madge and Gertrude, retired to the gym., where they were speedily joined by the Second Form delegates, Betty Oliver and Veronica Seton.

'It's just ten to two,' said Gwen nervously. 'It is not a pleasant ordeal to go to defy the captain when she happens to be your elder sister as well.'

'What are we going to say to them?'

'We'll tell them that we aren't going to fag unless they promise not to rag us,' returned Con, who was troubled by no such consideration.

'And we'll say that anyhow we aren't going to fag for the Fifth,' proposed Madge, who had been severely lectured only the day before by Joan Hethcote because she had forgotten to fetch the new blotting-paper she had been told to bring.

'All right! Are you all ready?—Tessa, you'll go first, won't you?'

'Yes, if you wish,' replied Tessa. 'But why not let the smallest go first?'

'Oh, good!—You've got to lead, then, Betty and Veronica! Oh, you don't have to talk! Just to go in!—Are you all ready? Come on, then! Let's get it over!'

And they set off for the prefects' room.

CHAPTER XVII.

THE ULTIMATUM.

TO say the prefects were startled when the delegates entered is to express it mildly.

'Of course, if we'd known you intended coming in a body, we'd have borrowed the Head's study!' said Marcia sarcastically.

The deputation wriggled uncomfortably. They felt it was unkind of Marcia to suggest that there were too many of them. Besides, it was all very well for the prefects to talk; there were sixteen of them, and they were in their own room. Perhaps the captain suddenly realised this, for she waved them to the chairs left vacant.

'Sit down,' she said. 'I'm afraid some of you will have to put up with the floor, but it can't be helped.'

The juniors sat down, and for two minutes there was solemn silence.

Then the captain spoke. 'Well,' she said, 'we are waiting! Why have you sent me this —er—communication? What is the trouble about?'

More shuffling and wriggling, combined with murmurs of 'You!'—'No, you!'—'Oh, go on, Gerry, you say it!'

'Who is the senior girl here?' demanded Marcia finally.

'Tessa is,' piped up Betty Oliver from the floor.

'Oh! Well, Tessa, of what do you people complain?'

Put like that, it sounded very judicial; and Tessa, with Concetta looking at her in an amused way, rose to her feet, looking very flushed. 'Well—er—it—er,' she stammered, and then stopped.

'Well,' said Marcia, after a moment or two, 'it's what? Go on!'

But it seemed to be beyond Tessa, who merely shuffled her feet.

'Oh, go on!' exclaimed Elsie impatiently. 'Don't "er" quite so much.'

Here Claire, who never could resist such a temptation, was overheard to murmur to Philippa, 'To *er* is human; to talk straight on divine,' which completely upset that young lady's risible faculties.

After a freezing look at the pair, Marcia turned to her sister. 'Well, Gwenna, can you elucidate matters any better?'

The blushing Tessa sat down gratefully;

G.S.   M

while Gwen, puzzled by the word 'elucidate,' and thrown off her balance by the unaccustomed use of her full name, floundered into an explanation which, as her elder sister impatiently expressed it, 'possessed neither sense nor meaning.'

It was left to Gerry to straighten out things, which she did by attacking the subject point-blank. 'Alicia and some of the others boss us about, and we aren't going to stand it any more, so we've struck!'

'Oh, indeed!' replied Marcia icily; while Gerry wondered how on earth she could be the same person as the Marcia who had been to tea at the Rectory on Saturday, and had been so jolly. However, she wasn't left to wonder for long, for Marcia's voice again broke the stillness: 'And is there anything else about which you wish to complain?'

'We—we think we oughtn't to have to report for changing shoes,' replied Gerry, blushing furiously.

'Indeed!'

It was all the comment Marcia made, but Gerry somehow felt as though she had been roundly scolded. Gwen broke in here. 'It isn't only Gerry,' she said defiantly. 'Don't rag her only, Marcia!'

Her sister looked at her, 'as though I was

a black beetle,' Gwen phrased it after. But Tessa, fired by this example, also got up. 'And I also, Marcia,' she said; 'I also am in this affair.'

'And what do you expect us to do?' asked Pauline suddenly.

There was a blank silence. To tell the truth, no one had foreseen that the Sixth might offer to do anything. Then Con spoke. 'I think the Fifth ought not to fag us,' she said firmly. 'The prefects are different; we don't mind them.'

'Thank you,' said Madeleine gravely. 'We are deeply indebted to you!'

Con coloured furiously, and Nell Trevennor suddenly took up the ball. 'I must say I think you kids have a good cheek to come to us at all!' she said stormily. 'But to speak in the way you have spoken—you especially, Gerry! And to Marcia! I think you ought to be sent to Coventry, the lot of you!'

At this point no less a person than Gertrude Trevennor chimed in. 'Well, if you *do* send us to Coventry, you still can't make us fag for you!'

'That will do, Gertrude,' said Marcia coldly. 'You are here as the member of a deputation, not for the purpose of being impertinent to a prefect!'

Gertrude subsided into crushed silence, but every one felt that what she had said was true. Matters were at a deadlock, and seemed likely to remain so.

Finally, after a brief consultation with Pauline and Elsie, Marcia spoke. 'You may go now; it is almost half-past two. We will think over what you have said, and let you know our decision later on.—Geraldine Challoner, please stay! I want you!'

There was no help for it. The others filed out, Con and Gwen contriving to squeeze her hand as they went past; then the door closed, and Gerry was left alone with the prefects. These august beings glanced uncertainly at the captain and then at her.

'It's all right,' said Marcia. 'You needn't stay if you don't want to. I just want to ask her one or two questions.'

'Oh, thanks, Marcia! Then, if you don't mind, I'll go to my practice,' replied Concetta, rising as she spoke.

'I suppose I'd better go, too,' observed Judith.

Olwen and Jessie followed her out, and then Pamela, Eileen, and Hazel vanished in the direction of the library. The others got up and formed into knots, talking in low undertones. Marcia put out her hand and pulled

Gerry to her. 'Now, child,' she said, 'will you tell me why you are in this? I know you've not been hockey fag to the Second Eleven, and you never come across any of us —you behave too well as a rule. Why are you in this? You are new, and you don't understand what you are doing; the others do. I don't want you to go into it with your eyes closed. Come, Gerry, what have you to strike against?'

Gerry felt the tears rise to her eyes; but she knew that, whatever happened, you must never cry, so she choked them back. 'I—I— it's the others, Marcia! I can't strike if they do because they are ill-treated. It wouldn't be—wouldn't be——'

'Wouldn't be what?' demanded Marcia.

The others had left the room now, and they two were alone.

'What you said the other day in hall about sticking to one's Order,' explained Gerry, rather wishing Marcia wouldn't look at her so kindly. It made it so frightfully difficult to be a man and not cry.

Perhaps the captain realised this, for she removed her gaze from the small, sensitive face as she said slowly, 'That's true, child. But supposing your Order is wrong, are you going to stick to it then?'

Gerry looked bewildered, so she explained further. 'Supposing you were a miner, and the men of your pit had formed a plan to murder all the people who held any responsible post in the pit, would you join them because you were of their Order?'

'N-no, Marcia,' replied Gerry slowly. Then she added quickly, 'But this is different. And—and, please, Marcia, if the others strike, I must!'

A gleam of admiration lit up Marcia's eyes for a moment. Then she dropped her hand from the small arm and rose to her feet. 'Very well,' she said; 'I have warned you! You may go now!'

Gerry turned, and went with laggard feet, the school captain looking after her with a curious expression on her fine face.

'Little brick!' she murmured to herself. 'That child would have made a fine martyr or a crusader!' Which proved that Marcia Compton was no mean reader of character.

In the form room, where her fellow-strikers were sitting sewing, Gerry was greeted with eager invitations to 'Come and sit down beside me!'

Miss Hildreth, the form-mistress of IV.B, took this lesson, and as long as the conversation was not too noisy she permitted it on the afternoons she did not read aloud to them. She now merely smiled at Gerry, with a cheery, 'Well, have the prefects finished with you?' and then turned to attend to Primrose Stevens, who was nearly in tears over her hem.

Gerry got out her petticoat and sat down beside Con and Muriel, who were all ears to hear what had happened when the rest of the delegates had left the room. However, they got no satisfaction, for Gerry refused to tell them, and turned the conversation on to the question of what would happen next.

'Goodness knows!' returned Muriel, as she stroked her gathers vigorously.

'Well, I don't think they'll give in,' said Con.—'Scissors, please, some one! Thank you!—You see, it's their own idea, this changing of shoes affair, isn't it? And they couldn't back down on it very well.'

'There'll be a fiendish row!'

Bettina Isherwood, a harum-scarum person, who happened to be sitting in front with her great chum, Janet Grant, turned round at this. 'There'll be a fiendish row!' she said. 'They'll get back on us somehow!'

'Yes; I s'pose they will,' agreed Con, as she patted her work on her knee and examined a buttonhole with great satisfaction.

'Con Atherton, let me see your work,' said Miss Hildreth at that moment.

Con produced it, and waited complacently for the praise she felt to be her just due. It never came. Instead, Miss Hildreth's eyes widened with horror. 'Con!' she exclaimed. 'Do you know what you've done? You've actually made a buttonhole on a single thickness of material! How long do you imagine it will last?'

'I don't know,' mumbled Con, blushing to the roots of her hair.

'Nor any one else!' replied the mistress. 'Well, it's too late to alter it now. Make the next one here, and do *think* for the future, child!—Muriel, what are *you* doing?'

'Stroking gathers,' explained Muriel, as she held up her night-dress for inspection.

'*Stroking* gathers! Are you sure you don't mean *cutting* them?' demanded Miss Hildreth. 'What are you using, may I ask?'

'This!' and Muriel held up a large darning-needle.

'A darning-needle! No wonder you are cutting the threads! How often must I tell you to stroke your gathers with a pin, and not to scratch? It seems to be waste of time for me to talk.—Geraldine, what are you after?' Gerry finished the list, for she was placidly hemming round her petticoat on the right side. Miss Hildreth groaned. 'I thought I could trust *you*! I think you must all have taken leave of your senses! Unpick it at once and start afresh! If this is the result of letting you talk, I shall forbid it for the future!' And she left them to attend to Mary Anderson, who had lost her last needle, and couldn't go on.

Left to themselves, the trio grinned at each other; and Bettina, turning round again, whispered, 'Well, it doesn't seem to worry you much!'

'It doesn't!' returned Con. 'Life's too short to bother about such things.'

'Less talking, Con, and more work!' called Miss Hildreth from the other side of the room. 'You are all talking too much!— Olive Purvis, run along to the staff-room and look on my shelf. You'll see a book with a dark-green back there called *A Little Princess*. Bring it to me, and I'll read to you.'

Olive ran off, and presently came back with the book, and for the rest of the lesson III.A sewed diligently, while Miss Hildreth read to them from the story of Sara Crewe and her dolls. When the three-quarters of an hour was up she just waited to see the work folded and returned to its drawer, and then she hurried off, and the Third clustered round Gerry.

'What did Marcia want, Gerry? Did she rag you at all?'

Mercifully for Gerry—for she had no intention of telling any one what Marcia had said—Miss Hamilton entered the room, and sternly called the form to order. There was nothing for it but to get out one's books and go on with preparation; and when four o'clock chimed, and they had all filed in orderly fashion down to the cloakroom, what they saw on the notice-board there made them forget everything else. Pinned up was a notice in Marcia's handwriting, and signed by the rest of the prefects:

'NOTICE.

'Until this absurd strike ceases, members of the school from and including Forms IV.B to II. are forbidden to use either the school library or the playing-fields. Walks will be arranged instead of hockey and lacrosse practices.'

The juniors were raging when they had taken this in.

'I'm going to Miss Catcheside!' declared Kitty O'Connell.

'No go!' groaned Gloria Fitzgerald. 'She's signed it, too! Look!' And there in the

left-hand corner was the well-known signature,
'Rotha M. Catcheside.'

The Lower School left that afternoon in
almost dazed silence. The prefects had certainly got home this time !

CHAPTER XVIII.

JILL GOES SKATING.

'YOU'RE awfully quiet, Gerry! What's the matter? You're as mum as a mouse to-night!'

'Nothing is the matter, Paul, honestly. And I've got heaps to do.'

Paul stretched himself, laughing, as he looked down at the little girl. 'You've changed, my kidlet! Only six weeks since you came, and you aren't the same girl. I wonder what your aunts will say?'

'Goodness knows!' returned Gerry impatiently. 'Do let me get on, Paul!'

He glanced at her curiously, opened his lips to say something, and then closed them again. Jill, at the other side of the table, watched them, with a contemptuous sneer spoiling her pretty mouth. Matters were no easier between her and Gerry. Not that they came across each other very much. Gerry had made great headway in her school work, and more than once Miss Hamilton had hinted that if she continued to improve as she was doing she would get her remove at Christmas.

Thanks to Paul, who had unexpectedly proved himself a born teacher, her mathematics were almost on a level with the rest of the form's. The bright, inspiring teaching which she was getting, and which was so different from that of Miss Sinclair of Dumberley days, was helping her as she had never been helped before. She was very keen to gain her remove, but there was one drawback attached to it. If she did, she would have to leave behind Con Atherton and Muriel Hatherley. Con, while clever at art, and the pride of the junior art master, otherwise possessed only average abilities; while Muriel, dear, sunshiny person as she was, contentedly occupied the bottom of the form week in and week out. The three people who would be likely to accompany Gerry at Christmas — Dorothy Ellis, Maidie Penrose, and Jean Ross— while they were very charming and all very friendly, were still not her chums, as the other two were. Of course, she would have Gwen and Tessa, and there would be Gloria Fitzgerald and Kitty O'Connell. Still, Gerry would have liked it better had Con and Muriel

been with her. Now she bent all her mind
to her work, and paid no more attention to
Paul, who was lounging on the piano-stool
playing idly any fragments that occurred
to him.

'How's the great strike going?' he queried
suddenly.

'Haven't you heard? It fizzled out,' Jill
told him scornfully. 'As soon as they saw
they were going to lose their games and story-
books they all backed down, and apologised to
Marcia next day!'

Gerry raised a flaming face. 'That's not
true, Jill, and you know it!'

''Tis true, then!' flashed Jill. 'Didn't you
delegate idiots go and tell them you were
sorry, and you'd be good little girls for ever-
more, after dinner on the Thursday?'

'No, we didn't! If you want to know, we
told them we felt it wasn't fair on the school
to cut games practice, and we'd stop striking;
but we said we still thought it wasn't fair that
the Fifth should fag us, or that they should
rag us; and we've none of us taken any books
out of the library since; so, now!'

Paul grinned to himself. Gerry was rapidly
finding her feet; she needed little care now,
and he was glad of it. He thought it better,
however, to change the subject, so he said,

'Birkett's Pond is holding, so I'm informed. What price a skating-party to-morrow afternoon?'

'Oh, ripping!' exclaimed Nell, who entered at that moment, just in time to overhear him. 'Marcia and Gwen and Madeleine are coming to tea, so it will be top-hole sport!'

'Why not the morning, too? Let's go to-morrow at ten, Paul! Oh, do!' coaxed Jill.

'Nothing doing! I'm playing in church on Sunday, so I've got to practise, and I can get Georgie to-morrow at nine to blow for me!'

'Well, but we can go by ourselves, can't we? And you could come to us?' suggested his sister, who was loath to give up her scheme.

'You must ask the pater about that,' returned Paul. 'I won't take any responsibility.'

Jill, seeing that he was determined, said nothing further, but returned to her geometry. Gerry was already buried fathoms deep in the reign of Mary of England; and Nell, with many sighs and groans, was struggling with a French essay. Sheila's lessons were finished, and she presently came trotting in to say that Paul was wanted at the door,

and as it was half-past seven, Gerry and Jill
had only another half-hour in which to work.
'An' I'm going to bed now,' she concluded.
'Good-night, every one!'

Then she danced away upstairs; the Rectory
children were not much given to kissing.
Paul sauntered out of the room after her,
and the two younger girls bent all their
energies to their tasks. It was the rule at
the Rectory that no one under fifteen might
do work after eight o'clock at night. If your
prep. was not finished then, it had to remain
unfinished. Nell and Larry were given an
extra half-hour, but, plead as they might,
Jill, Gerry, Bernard, and Cecil had to put
their books away as the clock chimed eight.
Jill, in particular, found this rule terribly
irksome. She was brilliantly clever, and intensely ambitious. Already she was in a form
where the average age was fifteen months
higher than her own; and it was whispered
at school among the girls that Jill Trevennor
should have been put into V.B, but Miss
Catcheside was afraid of overworking her.
Bernard, on the other hand, while very well-
meaning, was slow in the extreme. Cecil's
attendance at school was so intermittent that
up to the present the rule had not troubled
him. With Gerry came a new problem. She

had so much leeway to make up with regard to mathematics, and was so anxious to get on, that there had been tears more than once over the chiming of eight. Now, however, she was more used to things, and got through her work more quickly.

The chiming of eight o'clock brought about a catastrophe; for Jill, in her hurry to finish her work, made a wild dive at the ink-bottle at the same time as Nell, and between them it was upset, and the ink went over Nell's French essay. She looked at it in speechless horror; whilst Jill and Gerry, in accord for once, rushed at the precious screed with blotting-paper, and did their valiant best to right matters. But even when it had been dried most carefully, it was obvious that it could not be given in. Mademoiselle was not the most patient person in the world, and, as Nell said, she would probably dash straight off to Miss Catcheside with an ink-stained essay like that.

'There's nothing for it but recopying it to-morrow morning,' said its owner ruefully. 'Oh, it wasn't your fault, Jilly—at least, no more than it was mine. I certainly can't give it in like that.'

'I'm so sorry, Nell!' said Jill remorsefully. 'I wish I could do it for you!'

'Well, you can't! But it's decent of you, old thing! There's mother calling you and Gerry! *Scootez-vous, très vite!*'

Left to herself, Nell sighed, and then turned her attention to Cicero's *Pro Milone*. Presently Paul came in. 'Who was that?' she asked idly, as she hunted through a sentence to find the verbs.—'I wish they didn't shove the predicate at the end in Latin!—Who was it, Paul?'

'Maitland,' replied Paul. 'By the way, Nell, I'm not so sure that the skating stunt will come off after all. Maitland thinks it's inclined to thaw a bit, and the air does feel softer. You might tell the kids in case I forget, will you? Jill was saying something about going in the morning, and Birkett's Pond is pretty deep in places.'

'All right,' replied his sister, only half-hearing what he was saying. 'I say, Paul, you might give me a hand here, will you?'

Next morning, needless to state, neither Nell nor Paul remembered to tell their juniors about the thaw; Larry and Bernard were summoned to their father's study in order to help him to rearrange his books; Cecil shut himself up in his bedroom with his viola; Sheila went to the dining-room piano for her practice; and

Gerry, after she had made her bed and dusted the drawing-room with Nell, settled down at the piano there for an hour; Margaret was busy about the house; so Jill was left to her own devices. She wandered up to the nursery, but it was being 'turned out.' The two little ones were penned into a corner with chairs, and were enjoying themselves playing at 'lions.' But the game had no attraction for Jill, so she wandered out of the room again. In the dining-room Sheila was struggling valiantly with Mrs Curwen, while in the drawing-room Gerry was running lightly up and down the keys in scales whose smoothness and fluency were a perpetual source of joy to Signor Donati.

Jill felt dull. She went to the staircase window and gazed out, drumming on it with her fingers-tips, till Mary, the housemaid, came by, and somewhat tartly suggested that it was a pity Miss Jill could find nothing better to do than spoil other people's handiwork! Those windows had been cleaned only the day before !

Jill desisted, because she felt too bored even to argue. She went downstairs and along to the kitchen, where her mother was busy with cook. Obviously there was no room for her here. She went on into the scullery, and

gazed round. In the corner behind the step-
ladder were hung the skates. The gleaming
blades caught her eye. She looked at them;
then she looked out of the window. How
cold it was! It must be freezing ever so
hard! How lovely it would be on the pond!
A pity to disturb any one by asking for
permission! She seized her skates, and ran
back through the kitchen with them. As
she passed the drawing-room door Gerry
came out. She had discovered that she was
minus a handkerchief, and was going upstairs
for it.

'Hello! Are you going skating, Jill?' she
ventured.

'Mind your own business,' snapped Jill,
'and I'll mind mine!'

She ran along to the cloakroom and changed
into stout boots. Then she put on her big
coat and scarlet tam. At the last minute
prudence whispered that it was cold, and she
snatched a long woollen scarf from one of the
pegs and twisted it round her throat. Then
she let herself out, and ran through the garden
on to the road. A feeling of exhilaration took
hold of her. The keen, frosty air stung the
warm colour into her cheeks, and she danced
gaily along, the skates clanging on her arm.
She met no one, for the way to Birkett's Pond

lay mainly across the fields, lying white and silent under their covering of snow. In the clear, frosty air sound carried far and distinctly, and Jill could hear the twittering of a bird near the hedge. In common with the rest of the Rectory children she invariably carried crusts in her pocket when the ground was hard, and now she pulled one out, and, running towards the spot where she had heard the sound, she broke it into fragments ere she went on her way. Through another field she went, and then she crossed a little copse and came in sight of her goal. The pond lay black and still in its frame of white snow, and the sight of the ice thrilled her. This would be the first skating since last December. An old tree-trunk gave her a seat, and she put her skates on quickly and deftly, stamping when she had got them on to warm her feet. It took her a very few minutes to stagger down to the lake, and then—oh, the joy of the exercise !

Like most of the Rectory children Jill was a good skater, and she struck out boldly round the outside first; then, turning, she made for the centre, where the water was very deep, and where the ice looked smoother. Suddenly she heard a long, sharp 'cr-r-rack !' which struck cold terror to her heart. She knew well what that meant, and made a valiant effort to swing round. Too late! Her skate sank in the rotten ice, and with a dreadful crash it gave, and she sank down, down, down, into black icy water.

CHAPTER XIX.

THE RESCUE.

WHEN she came downstairs with her handkerchief, Gerry went slowly back to the drawing-room. It was a quarter to ten, and she still had twenty minutes' practice to do. But something seemed to be quenching all her pleasure in the music, and, though her fingers were moving over the keys in a Beethoven sonata, her mind was far away. It was for this reason, perhaps, that she overheard Paul when he came into the hall very much disgruntled.

'Peggy, the boys and I are going for a walk. That little ass Georgie has sprained something! What is it? How should I know? I'd like to wring his beastly little neck for him! No use attempting to practise now!—Ready, you kids?'

A chorus of 'Rather!' sounded.

Then Margaret's pretty notes, 'Paul, what about the skating this afternoon?'

'Oh, that! No go! It thawed through

the night! Freezing hard again now, but the pond won't be safe. So-long!'

The front-door banged, and the sound of Margaret's footsteps died away down the passage. In the drawing-room Gerry sat very still, while her brain took in the awfulness of what she had only half-consciously heard. The pond wasn't safe, and Jill had gone skating! It was deep, too! Gerry remembered that Paul had told her of how a blind man, new to the district, and new to blindness, had once strayed out of the path and nearly got drowned in it. It was ten feet deep in some places, and Jill was there. She was there alone, and no one knew but Gerry herself.

It was at this point that Gerry's stunned mind began to wake up. Oddly enough, no idea of telling any one else came to her. She said afterwards that all she could think of was Jill and that awful water. Rising quickly, she left the room, went to the cloakroom, and put on her coat and tam; a hockey-stick stood in one corner, and some instinct bade her take it. The same instinct set her to catch up a pair of gloves, though she did not stop to change her shoes. Then she let herself out of the front-door as quietly as Jill had done some thirty minutes before, and hurried out

of the garden and down the road. She knew
the way over the fields, and she went on
unfalteringly until she came to the one where
Jill had stopped to give crusts to the birds.
Here there was a stile, with three paths
leading from it. Gerry was puzzled as to
which to choose. A ploughboy had gone
along after Jill, and his footprints obliterated
hers. For a minute the little girl pondered;
then, as she looked round, her eye was caught
by the crusts, and she gave a great sob of
thankfulness, for they indicated which way
Jill had gone. She tore down the slope of
the field, the feathery snow-dust flying behind
her feet, and through the copse, and as she
reached the middle of it she heard the sound
of a scream, which froze her heart. With
great sobs choking her, and a sharp pain
catching her side, Gerry stumbled on, and
reached the pond. There, almost in the
centre of it, her hands clutching frantically
at the rotten ice, which crumbled beneath
her desperate clutch, was Jill. Her tam had
vanished, and her thick, short hair was wet;
her face was ghastly, and her eyes held a
terror which gave Gerry fresh pain, so agonised
was it. At all costs she must relieve that
fear. Dread of what she might find and panic-
stricken speed had combined to rob her of

well-nigh all her breath. But she managed to give vent to a shriek of, 'Jill, hold on! I'm coming!'

Jill heard her. She turned her head and saw her.

Gerry came cautiously across the ice, and then Jill did one of the finest deeds of her life. 'Gerry, keep back!' she gasped. 'It's all rotten!'

But Gerry did not need the warning. It had been blind instinct which had made her catch up the hockey-stick; now she used her reason. The groaning of the ice warned her that she must not attempt to go farther on her feet. Lying down on her face, she began to worm her way along, until she was able to thrust the crook of the hockey-stick within Jill's reach. Quick to guess her idea, Jill grasped it, and then part of Gerry's nerve went. Lying there, with only a hockey-stick between Jill and certain death, she screamed in a perfect frenzy of terror, screamed until it seemed to both children that her cries must be heard in Dawley itself. But no one came, and the ghastly minutes crept by, each an hour in length.

The deathly cold was beginning to tell on Jill. Her eyes half-closed, and a grayish pallor stole over her face; only her fingers

clutched rigidly at the stick. To Gerry,
already half-distraught, she looked dead.
The poor child thought that she was dead,
and the awful fear of having to spend the day
there with a dead person nearly drove her mad.
But no thought of letting go entered her head.
Once again she raised her voice in a series
of agonised screams. Farmer Birkett, nearly
half a mile away, heard them, and dropped his
hammer to rush into the house and get a coil
of rope and a ladder before he started through
the woods, accompanied by two hinds, whom
he pressed into service. Paul, bringing his
brothers to the pond by another way, heard
them, and set off at his best speed. Mr
Maitland, striding down the road on an errand
of mercy, heard them, and vaulted the hedge,
and tore across the fields as if his life depended
upon it. Paul got there first, Farmer Birkett
made a good second, and the rest came up
panting. In almost less time than it takes
to tell they had the step-ladder down, and two
of the men held on to the ends of it, while
Paul crept along with the coil of rope round
his neck. He dared not go close to Jill—his
weight was too much—but he gripped the
hockey-stick firmly, and gave the rope to
Gerry. It had been made into a big noose
at one end, and this she contrived to throw

over Jill's shoulders. By this time Larry and Mr Maitland were ready, and Paul contrived to edge Gerry along into safety. A few minutes more, and Jill, gray, still, and to all appearance dead, lay on the bank beside Gerry. Mr Maitland dragged off her shoes and stockings and frock, and he and Paul rubbed her arms and legs with snow until the skin was red. Then they rubbed her back and chest, and gradually the gray look left her face and a little colour came to her lips. Then the curate desisted. Picking up his overcoat, which he had flung off the better to work, he rolled her up in it, and then, lifting her as though she were a baby, he turned to Paul. 'Fetch the other kid!' he said. 'Make her walk if she can!'

Paul tried to set Gerry on her feet; but the cramped muscles refused to do their duty, so he picked her up in his arms and set off in his friend's footsteps, accompanied by the farmer, who had sent one of his men in advance to warn Mrs Trevennor. Of that walk neither of the young men would speak for days. They met no one on the fields, and along the high-road were only a tramp and the boys, whom Paul had sent on. As they turned into the lane they saw Mrs Trevennor hastening towards them, her face white, and her eyes shining.

'My Jilly!' she said, and would have taken the unconscious girl out of Mr Maitland's arms, but he refused to let her go.

'It's all right, Mrs Trevennor! Don't worry! She'll be all right once she gets into bed and has something hot to drink. I'll just carry her up; she's too heavy for you.'

Upstairs he carried her, into the big attic bedroom she shared with Nell, and there he laid her down on her little white bed, while Paul laid Gerry on Nell's.

'Get them undressed,' said Mr Maitland. 'Larry's gone for the doctor in case of need, Mrs Trevennor.'

Then he and Paul left the room, to rush to the bathroom and fetch cans of hot water. Nell was rushing round with blankets heated at the kitchen fire, and cook boiled enough milk to have served a crèche full of babies.

At last the doctor arrived, and Mr Maitland breathed more freely. He felt nervous as to the effects of the shock on both children. But there was no need for worry; for when the old gentleman, who had known the Trevennor children nearly all their lives, came downstairs, he was accompanied by Mrs Trevennor, and one look at her face told the two young men that all was well.

'Quite all right, ye rascals!' chuckled the doctor, rubbing his hands gleefully. 'Now, barring a bad cold—and I'm hoping they may get off that, ye were so prompt—they ought to do. They've had a shock, but that's punishment to the young imps for going where they weren't allowed to go! Maitland, ye've a head on your shoulders! Your wife, when you get her, will be a lucky woman— eh, Mrs Trevennor?' And he went off, still chuckling.

Mrs Trevennor came forward and took the young man's hands in hers. 'Oh, Mr Maitland,' she said earnestly, 'we owe the children's lives—certainly Jill's life—to you! I feel I can never repay you for this! If ever I can do anything for you——'

Suddenly she broke off, for Mr Maitland's face was telling her that there was, indeed, something she could do for him. 'Come into the dining-room,' she said in altered tones. 'Go home to lunch?' as he made a feeble protest. 'Indeed, you can't! You must stay here to lunch! The rector was called to Dawley very unexpectedly this morning, and I don't expect him back till tea-time. I know he wants to see you, so you must wait.—Paul, please go and ask Mary to hurry up.'

Paul vanished, and then Mrs Trevennor

turned to her guest. 'You will excuse me, won't you? I feel I can't bear to have them out of my sight for a moment! You do understand?'

'Oh, rather!' he said. 'I'm sure you do!'

She vanished, and he was left alone. But not for long. Five minutes later Margaret entered the room, a wonderful light in her eyes, and came up to him. 'Mr Maitland, oh, I can't thank you enough! I only wish there was something I could do to show you how much I do thank you!'

Mr Maitland looked at her as she stood there in all the glory of her girlish beauty. 'There is something,' he said, and told her what it was.

That conversation has nothing to do with us, so we will ignore it; but ten minutes later Paul entered the room to find his pretty sister in the arms of his father's curate. Both were too much occupied to see him, so he slipped out quietly, and raced upstairs to tell his mother, who was sitting watching by the two beds where Gerry and Jill were sleeping peacefully.

'Is that all?' she said calmly when he had told her his news in excited but low tones. 'I thought you had something fresh to tell me, you were so excited. I knew all about it!'

'You women!' groaned Paul. Then he looked at the little sleepers. 'Anyhow, it'll be news to the kids and the pater! Bags me to tell it!'

CHAPTER XX.

MAKING UP.

WHEN you have studiously kept up a feud with a person for nearly two months, when you have gone out of your way to be nasty to her and hated her with all your heart, it is rather a difficult matter to make things up, more particularly when you have to be the person to say you are sorry. Jill was finding this out. During the week that followed her adventure she had ample time for thought. The prolonged immersion in icy water had brought on a severe chill, and for two or three days she was too ill even to think. Then, as she got better, conscience reproached her for her treatment of the guest who had come to them.

As she reviewed her conduct of the past weeks, it seemed to her that she must have been possessed by a demon. The hot colour flooded her face as she remembered the episode of the midnight battle. She could recall other events, too, of which she now felt bitterly ashamed—that first Monday morning

in the train when she had turned her back on
Gerry and talked to Naïda; time after time
when she had sneered at the visitor's way of
speaking and behaving; time after time at
school when she might have helped, and
didn't; even that dreadful morning of the
accident, when she had snapped Gerry up.
And Gerry hadn't borne malice! Far from
it! She had rushed away on hearing of her,
Jill's, danger, and had even risked her own
life. For Paul said afterwards that it was
only a miracle which had saved Gerry from
going through as well. Jill had proved herself a good hater; but she was also a good
lover. Now she simply burned to show
how sorry she was for all that she had
done.

But Gerry, who had escaped almost scot-
free, was at school most of the day, where,
much to her embarrassment, she was treated
as a heroine. For Sheila and Nell had spread
the news of her daring broadcast; and Miss
Catcheside had alluded to it at prayers on the
morning when she asked them to thank God
for the safety of one of their members whose
life had been in the gravest peril. 'Peril,'
continued the headmistress, 'which only the
self-possession and courage of another girl
averted. Had Geraldine Challoner not kept

her head as she did, we might have been mourning the loss of Gillian Trevennor. As it is, both are alive, and Gillian is recovering from the effects of her accident, so that in a short time we may hope to have both of them amongst us, thank God!'

Gerry had alternately paled and blushed during this speech; and as for III.A, its members were nearly bursting with pride—so much so, in fact, that they found it impossible to bother about such a commonplace thing as work, and were awarded extra repetition in consequence.

At home, too, Gerry was in much demand. She had her home lessons in the evenings; and although she came each evening to say 'Good-night' when Sheila did, there was always some one there, and Jill felt that she could not speak in front of others.

So the week wore away, and when Sunday came matters still stood where they had been. Jill was to sit up for the first time that day, and she was to have a tea-party, which should include the entire family. Somehow she felt that she must settle things before tea-time. As the morning wore on she became so restless and irritable that Mrs Trevennor, fearing that the excitement was proving too much for her, turned Nell out, lowered the blinds, and bade her invalid try to sleep. Then she herself left the room.

But sleep was far enough from Jill. Restlessly she tossed and turned, until the bed looked like a haystack, and the sheets and blankets were all untucked at the bottom. From downstairs she could hear her father's voice summoning his flock to get ready for church ere he departed himself. She heard the sound of feet on the stairs, the carefully lowered voices as they passed her room, the sound of the front-door closing, and then the merry chatter gradually dying away as they went down the road. There was silence in the house after that, and she actually did fall asleep. She was wakened by a patter of tiny feet, and opened her eyes to see Baby Betty standing on tiptoe by the bed.

'Jill! Jill! Wake up! Me wants to 'peak to 'oo! Jill!'

'Climb up, darling!' said Jill, raising herself up on her elbow. 'Come along!'

Betty clambered up, and curled herself into a snug little bundle within Jill's arm. Then she patted the short, dark hair with little dimpled hands. 'Poor Jill! Me are so sowwy for 'oo, Jill! Shall me tell 'oo a 'torwy?'

'Oh yes, do,' replied Jill with flattering enthusiasm. 'I love your stories!'

Highly delighted with herself, Betty gripped one of her sister's hands firmly in both of hers, and, nodding her head till all her curls bobbed again, began. 'Once zere was a little boy, an' he had no clo'es!' Here the narrator stopped and looked at her audience.

Jill rose to the occasion at once. 'No! How dreadful!' she said. 'Whatever did he do?'

'Zat's ze 'torwy,' replied Betty with dignity. 'He had no clo'es, an' his muzzer said, "Doe to bed at once!" An' he went!'

'What happened then?' asked Jill with interest.

'Zat's all! Now you tell me one!'

'Which one?' Jill temporised.

'I don't know. Oh yes, ze one about ze bears!'

Jill plunged straight away into the adventures of Curlylocks, while the baby sat clutching her sister's hand. When the story was finished, there was silence for a minute or two. Jill was trying to make up her mind to something, and Betty was absorbed in pulling the fringe out of the edge of the counterpane, which happened to be one of the old-fashioned 'honeycomb' kind. Suddenly the older girl made up her mind.

'Betty,' she said, cuddling that small person

close to her, 'will you do something for poor
Jill?   A big secret, Betty, darling, just for
you and me and Gerry?'

Betty adored secrets. She was very fond
of trotting round to her brothers and sisters
and whispering lengthy and totally inaudible
sentences in their ears, always ending up with,
'An' it's a big sec'et!' So now she squeezed
down beside her sister in an ecstasy of delight,
and rubbed her curls well into Jill's mouth in
her anxiety to hear it.

'I wan't you to ask Gerry to come to see
me,' said Jill softly. 'Just as soon as she
comes in, Betts, tell her I want her, will you?
And don't let any one else hear, and don't tell
any one else, 'cos it's a big secret!'

'Big, big sec'et,' murmured Betty ecstati-
cally. She bent down and kissed Jill to the
accompaniment of a fierce hug. Then she
sat up suddenly. 'Zey're coming!'

The sound of the merry voices came up
clearly, borne on the still, frosty air, for since
the disastrous Saturday morning the frost had
held, and the Ice King had the land in his
iron grip, only relaxing a little during the
whole of the Wednesday, when it had snowed
unceasingly all day and night.

With a final hug Betty scrambled down
and trotted out of the room, bursting with the

importance of her 'sec'et,' and Jill was left alone.

Five minutes later there was a tap at the door, and then Gerry entered, looking rather scared, and closed it carefully behind her. When Betty, clutching her hand, and with every hair on her head dancing in wild confusion, had begged her to 'Come an' have a sec'et,' she had imagined it would be one of the usual affairs, and had followed the small messenger into the drawing-room without any thought of what was to come. But when Betty had contrived to whisper, 'Jill wants 'oo! Now!' she had felt breathless with surprise. It couldn't be true!

'All right, darling,' she said to the baby.

But that young person was determined to see her up the stairs.

'Doe on!' she said with a push. 'She said "now."'

'But—but, baby, darling, it isn't really true?' asked poor bewildered Gerry.

Betty's mouth drooped ominously. 'Now!' she insisted. 'Doe 'way, Gewwy! She said "now."'

Convinced at last, Gerry slowly left the room and mounted the stairs. What could Jill want with her? She opened the door and slipped into the room. Jill was lying back on her pillows, looking very white and frail—a very different Jill from the impish person she had known. Gerry went up to her bedside, wondering what she wanted.

Now, while she had waited, Jill had been manufacturing beautiful sentences, in which she humbly apologised for her former rudeness and unkindness, and begged Gerry to forgive her and be friends. But when she saw her rescuer standing looking at her with big anxious eyes all her speech slipped away from her memory, and she could only hold out her arms, crying, 'Oh, Gerry! Gerry!'

Gerry's response was prompt. She tumbled on to the bed, and the two girls clung together in a hug which said far more than the most eloquent speech could have done. Presently they sat up, and Jill began to explain. 'Oh, Gerry, I've wanted to be friends all this week! And I just couldn't say it when the others were there! And you never came alone! I've been a horrid, jealous pig, Gerry dear! But I *am* sorry.'

'It doesn't matter a bit,' returned Gerry; 'and it was as much my fault as yours. I used to hang round Paul on purpose, 'cos I knew you didn't like it, and I wanted to vex you! So it was my fault, you see.'

But this Jill would not allow. 'You

haven't been half as much to blame as I have! You were our guest, and Paul was right that night when he said he was ashamed of me! Can you ever forgive me, Gerry? I banged your head hard, I know!'

'Well, I made your nose bleed!' returned Gerry cheerfully. And then suddenly, for the first time, the funny side of that affair struck her, and she burst out laughing. Jill eyed her doubtfully for a minute, and then she, too, began to laugh.

'Ho! ho! ho! Oh, Gerry, how funny you looked with your nighty-collar all hanging loose at one side, and your hair all anyhow!'

'And you, Jill! Yours was all on end as if you'd had a fright, an' the blood had streaked your face, an' you looked like a Red Indian!'

'An' when the clothes wrapped us up, an' we couldn't get free!'

'And, oh, how mad Paul was! He shook us when he picked us up!'

At this point Paul himself marched into the room. He stared at them, as well he might. It was a new state of affairs to see Jill and Gerry sitting clutching at each other and screaming with laughter. At the sight of his face the two girls redoubled their shrieks of mirth, till Mrs Trevennor, attracted by the noise, came on the scene.

'Jill! Gerry!' she gasped. Then, with a sudden twinkle, 'There isn't much wrong with you, Gillian, my child, when you can laugh like that. Back to school you go next week! I'll have no more malingering now!'

The sound of the gong called them to dinner, and she chased Paul and Gerry out of the room and downstairs.

In the dining-room the rector had been carving delicately for Jill. When the tray was ready Nell rose to carry it upstairs, but her mother stopped her.

'It's all right, dear,' she said, her eyes dancing with suppressed merriment at the thought of the bomb she was about to explode in her family. 'Gerry will carry it up; won't you, Gerry?'

'Rather!' replied Gerry enthusiastically. She picked up the tray and started for the door.

Sensation!

CHAPTER XXI.

CHUMS AT LAST.

THE following week Jill returned to school. During that week she and Gerry had become fast friends, and it is to be feared that Gerry's home lessons were somewhat scamped; for who could think about geography, and algebra, and Latin grammar when Jill was waiting to be talked to? Nell declared despairingly that it was no longer possible to do her lessons in her bedroom—there was always too much noise going on. She took to sitting in Gerry's room, and then, on the Friday, Mrs Trevennor made a suggestion which charmed every one concerned.

'Why not let Nell and Gerry change rooms? It would really be far better for the two younger girls to be together, and Nell needs a room to herself nowadays. What do you think?'

They all hailed the suggestion with delight; so Saturday was spent in transferring Nell's possessions downstairs and Gerry's upstairs, and when everything was settled Jill and

Gerry danced round the room together, ending up by bumping their heads against the sloping ceiling, which somewhat curbed their high spirits.   Then they had all gone out for a walk ; and in the afternoon Marcia and Gwen, Madeleine, Claire, and Naïda, had come to tea, and they had had a fine snowballing match with the boys, in which Geoff had somehow contrived to bury himself in the snowdrift, whence he had been dug out with shrieks of laughter, which so offended him that he stalked away to the house in high dudgeon, and refused to return.

The Monday which saw Jill's return to school was rather an embarrassing one for her.   Her own Form nearly overwhelmed her with questions as soon as ever she entered the cloakroom.   Then Miss Catcheside had sent for her, and welcomed her back among them. The juniors had all stared at her with wide-open eyes.

'Just as though I were a show!' said Jill indignantly.

However, the term was rapidly nearing its end ; any spare time was given up to rehearsals of the two great plays, and the excitement soon died down.   At any moment, when you entered any room, you would see at least half the girls present conning their parts over and over. The seniors, it is true, were not quite so openly excited as the juniors, but still an atmosphere of tension pervaded the whole school.

Gerry, who, to her great glee, had been allotted the part of a sea-fairy, neglected a good many things in order to practise her solo dance; Gwen, who was playing Tom, the chimney-sweep, had no time for such mundane things as lessons; and even Louie Baker of the Lower Sixth, who was to be Mrs Be-done-by-as-you-did, spent her time practising her song, 'I once had a sweet little doll, dears.'

The concert was to be divided into two parts. *The Water-Babies* would be played in the afternoon, and then the school would entertain all those parents who cared to stay for tea, and after tea and art and handicraft inspection would come Laurence Housman's play, *Prunella*.

As Nell Trevennor said laughingly, all the beauty and talent of the Upper School had been drawn on for this, one of the most ambitious things they had ever attempted. Concetta, of course, played the title-rôle; Nell herself was Pierrot; Pauline, Madeleine, and Marcia were the three maiden aunts; Peggy Hughes, a slim, boyish-looking girl from the

Upper Fifth, was Scaramel; Elsie Meredith, Olwen Tudor, and Rosemary Drewe were the gardeners; Nina Ruffell, from the Remove, played the gardener's boy; Pamela Hethcote and Hazel Burnham were the maids; and some of the Sixth and Fifth were the mummers. Cupid was to be played by Rosamund Atherton; and there was much conversation about dresses and scenery, all of which were being designed and manufactured by the Arts and Handicrafts Guilds. The school orchestra would play appropriate music; and Molly O'Farrell, happy possessor of an exquisite soprano voice, was to sing the tenor.

Certain of the older girls had to take part in *The Water-Babies*, playing such parts as 'the Squire' and Mrs Do-as-you-would-be-done-by. In the Lower School there were water-babies, sea-fairies, sea-creatures galore; Fiam ma Vivalanti, the baby of the Second, was a gorgeous dragon-fly; and to Allegra Atherton fell the part of 'Ellie' as a little girl. The grown-up 'Ellie' and 'Tom' of the last scene were played by Letty Harrison of IV.B and Sue Stevenson of V.A.

The staff were quite as much excited as were the girls; and even Miss Catcheside caught the infection, and made contributions of such gorgeous things as a pair of glinting blue-and-green wings for the dragon-fly, three real crinolines for the aunts, and a complete Cupid's dress, which just fitted Rosamund Atherton as though it had been made for her.

The days flew past, till at last the Day itself arrived. By that time every one was rather cross and tired. Dress-rehearsal the day before had gone badly. No one knew her lines or her place; Concetta's crinoline refused to work properly; while Madeleine, the stately, had tripped up over her unaccustomed long skirt and fallen headlong into Marcia's arms, much to the delighted amusement of the juniors who were present at the rehearsal. The tenor had cracked most unexpectedly on all his best top notes; while Claire Ashe, usually one of the most exquisitely graceful people imaginable, blundered over her solo dance in a way which made Madame Karanski, the dancing-mistress, wring her hands in horror. The climax had been reached when Allegra Atherton suddenly exclaimed that she had forgotten all her lines, and, bursting into tears, made straight for Rosamund's sheltering arms. Miss Hildreth, who was responsible for *The Water-Babies*, was very much upset; and, altogether, it had been what Gwen Compton tersely expressed as a 'wash-out.'

The prefects sat in their room, gloomily discussing the events of the final dress-rehearsal, at ten o'clock in the morning.

'If things don't go any better to-day I shall commit suicide,' vowed Claire, with as long a face as they had ever seen her pull.

'Don't be so absurd!' returned Marcia coldly.

'Well, you wait! I'll come and haunt you when I've nothing better to do,' laughed Claire, who could always be relied on to turn up smiling sooner or later.

'Oh, do be sensible!' wailed Olwen Tudor, who was hunting frantically amongst a pile of old exercise-books under the impression that her copy of *Prunella* was there.

'If you're looking for that beastly book of yours——' began Nell, when she was stopped by the entrance of Miss Catcheside.

The headmistress was smiling, and she had an air of mysterious delight about her. 'May I come in?' she asked. 'Or are you talking secrets?'

'Oh, do come in, Miss Catcheside!' exclaimed half-a-dozen voices; while Marcia, hastily rising, offered her chair.

Miss Catcheside sat down, looked round at them all with a beaming smile, and then exploded her bombshell. 'Girls, I've some news for you! Miss Hamilton is leaving us this term, rather unexpectedly.'

There was silence for a moment. Then Marcia spoke. 'I hope Miss Hamilton isn't ill, Miss Catcheside?'

Miss Catcheside's eyes danced with merriment as she replied, 'No; Miss Hamilton is not ill. She is merely engaged to be married!'

'Married! Miss Hamilton! Who to?'

'"Who to?" Nell! What grammar! It is to a Mr Lorrimer. I believe some of you know him by name?' The headmistress looked round inquiringly.

'I do,' replied Nell, completely unabashed by the rebuke she had just received. 'He is Cecil's maths. master. I have heard the boys talking about him.'

'And I,' added Marcia. 'My brother was under him for maths. He coached Arthur when he was working for his Little Go.'

'Well, I expect you are all busy,' smiled Miss Catcheside, rising, 'so I will go now. Don't worry too much about yesterday's fiasco.'

She left them, but she had left behind her news which far exceeded in importance even the plays. In less than half-an-hour it was all over the school; and an hour later a blushing, and angry, Miss Hamilton was half-laughingly accusing her chief of unfairness.

'My dear girl,' replied Miss Catcheside, 'it was too good an opportunity to be lost; you will see, the plays will go brilliantly now.'

And, indeed, it was afterwards acknowledged on all sides that St Peter's had excelled itself this time. Never, surely, had there been a more bewitching Prunella or whimsical Pierrot. Aunt Privacy brought tears to the eyes of the more susceptible of the girls; and Mrs Trevennor, sitting next to Mrs Atherton, murmured congratulations on Rosamund's playing of Cupid.

'And Pierrot!' laughed beautiful Mrs Atherton, who looked far too young to be the mother of such a big girl as Rosamund. 'He—she—oh, which is it? Anyhow, the acting is simply charming!'

But the climax was reached at the end of the evening, when Miss Hamilton, who was helping to shift scenes, suddenly found herself deserted on the stage.

The curtain went up, and then Marcia, blushing furiously, and looking, head girl as she was, most horribly embarrassed, came on with a beautiful bouquet, and stammered a few words of congratulation on behalf of the whole school.

Miss Hamilton turned even redder than Marcia, albeit the visitors had all gone, and there was only the school to witness the presentation, and, after thanking the captain, left the stage with all haste.

'Isn't it gorgeous?' whispered Jill, as she took Gerry's arm preparatory to following Nell and Marcia to the station. 'Where's Gwen, and Rosamund, and the others?—Oh, here you are! Hasn't it been a ripping finish off to the term?'

'Rather!' replied Gwen. 'Hi, Marcia, if you go at that rate, we can't keep up!'

'Oh, do be quick, you tiresome little things!' retorted Marcia, nevertheless slackening her pace a little. 'We shall miss the train!'

But they didn't.

That night, as Gerry was climbing into bed, Jill called across the room, 'Gerry, hasn't it been a glorious day?'

'The gloriousest ever!' replied Gerry.

'Gerry, there couldn't be a better!'

However, an even better day was to come.

CHAPTER XXII.

AFTER the great excitement of the concert, breaking-up day seemed tame, and
not even the news that she was promoted
to IV.B affected Gerry very much. There
were not many removes this term. Concetta
Donati was promoted to the Upper Sixth, and
Peggy Hughes and Alicia Brett had attained
to the Lower Sixth. In the Lower School,
Dorothy Ellis, Maidie Penrose, Jean Ross,
and Gerry Challoner were to go into IV.B,
and Madge Hannay and Allegra Atherton
into III.A. From the Second Form came
Daphne Hethcote, Rosalie Southern, Lilian
Ellis, Myfanwy Owen, and Joan Hannay, all
of whom looked very important when Miss
Catcheside read out their names.

When the last list was read, and the last
echo of the clapping had died away, Miss
Catcheside looked at the girls with her gayest
smile. 'It has been a very happy term, girls,
hasn't it?' she said. 'Now, before I wish

you happy holidays, I have two pieces of news for you. First of all, Tessa Donati has won an open exhibition offered by Sir Edward Burnham, Hazel's father, to the best performer on the violin. This exhibition will take Tessa to the Royal Academy of Music in two years' time when she is sixteen, and will pay all her expenses there for three years. If she does well, Sir Edward will give her an additional two years abroad. I am sure you are all as proud of Tessa as I am,' she went on smilingly. 'She has done brilliantly, for she was the youngest of fifty-seven competitors.' Here she was interrupted by a storm of cheering as the girls turned to look at Tessa, who, flushed and starry-eyed with excitement, for once outvied her lovely cousin in looks. For a minute or two the headmistress stood watching the tumult. Then she held up her hand for silence. When once more the hall was quiet she spoke again. 'One more piece of news. We have secured the field behind our playing-fields, and the men are going to start work on it at once, so that in the summer term we shall have eight additional tennis-courts for you.'

Here was news indeed, and the girls showed their hearty appreciation of it 'in the usual way.'

When at length the excitement had calmed down somewhat Miss Catcheside finally wished them a very happy Christmas, and then they all sang together the St Peter's end-of-term hymn.

After hand-shaking—and kissing, where the more popular mistresses were concerned—they streamed out to the cloakrooms, where they put on their outdoor things, and then said 'good-bye' to the school premises for four glorious weeks.

'Come on, Gerry,' called Gwen; 'let's make a bolt for an empty carriage!—Hi, Jill Trevennor, are you coming?'

For answer Jill joined them with a rush, and they all tore down the drive to the gate, where they were met by Marcia, Nell, Madeleine, Claire, and Philippa.

'Now, then,' said the captain sharply, 'be very careful, you children! Where are the Athertons?'

'Coming!' called Rosamund at this point. 'Sorry, Marcia, but we couldn't find Josie!'

'All right,' said Marcia. 'Now go quietly forward. You can't race through Dawley like mad things.' Which rather neatly frustrated Gwen's little plan to 'make a bolt for an empty carriage.'

'Poor kids!' laughed Claire; 'they were all ready for a bold dash to the railway station!'

'All the same,' said Madeleine, 'it wouldn't do. You're quite right, Marcia!'

However, once they were safely in the train the captain relaxed her vigilance, and the juniors were left to themselves, while their elders discussed the question of the new tennis-courts.

In the next carriage, Gerry, Jill, Rosamund, Con, Naïda, Muriel, and Gwen were comparing notes about parties.

'I've got four invitations already,' exulted Muriel—'yours, Rosamund, and Gwen's, and Kitty's, and the Kearneys'.'

'We're having one too,' chimed in Naïda, a pretty, fair-haired child of fourteen, who was generally very quiet and inconspicuous. 'Claire and Vivien and I are going to write the invitations this afternoon.'

'And we're going to have one after New Year,' added Gwen. 'And I know the Southerns are going to give one, *and* the Fitzgeralds.'

'And there's our skating-party.' Jill took up the tale. 'And the decorating, and the Sunday School Christmas-tree, and—oh, heaps of things! Isn't Christmas going to be jolly this year?—Gerry, aren't you glad you're with us?'

'Rather!' replied Gerry. 'And I've got such a gorgeous idea! Let's go carol-singing on Christmas Eve!'

Her suggestion was hailed with shrieks of delight.

'We can come over quite early,' said Con; 'and Muriel can come with us. Daddy shall fetch us in the car; and you, too, Naïda!'

'We'll sing all the carols we know, and have a collection,' added Muriel, 'and give all the money we get to the Shoeless Children's Fund!'

'Won't it be topping?'

'Gerry, you *ripper*!'

'Are you kids going to spend the rest of your lives in the train?' asked Nell Trevennor's voice at this point. 'Buck up and tumble out!' Thus adjured, Jill, Gerry, and Gwen 'tumbled out,' and joined the others on the platform just as the train moved out of the station.

'We didn't know we had stopped,' apologised Jill. 'Gerry's got a splendid idea. Let's go carol-singing on Cristmas Eve and collect money for the Shoeless Children's Fund. Isn't it gorgeous?'

'It's most excellent,' returned Marcia cordially.

Gerry blushed with pleasure at this acknowledgment from her idol; and when, on the way up to the Rectory, the big girls discussed it with their juniors in the most friendly manner, it seemed to her as though life could give her nothing more.

At the Rectory they said 'Good-bye' to Marcia and Gwen, and then raced each other through the snowy garden up to the front-door. They were met there by Cecil and Bernard, who had come home by an earlier train. They seemed to be bursting with suppressed excitement; but all Bernard said was, 'Gerry, they want you in the study. Buck along, my infant!'

With a startled look Gerry hurried to the study door and tapped.

'Come in, dear,' said the rector's voice.

She went in, and found him sitting by the fire, an open letter in his hand. Beside him, perched on the arm of his chair, was Mrs Trevennor, and as the little girl entered she sprang up and held out her arms. 'Gerry, darling,' she cried breathlessly, 'would you like to go back to Dumberley to your aunts?'

Gerry had run straight into those loving

arms. Now she drew back a little. Go back to Dumberley? But, then, she would miss all the fun and all the pleasure of the holidays. There would be no more St Peter's; no more jolly times with the others; above all, no more Jill. 'Oh,' she cried, 'I'm *not* ungrateful, and I *do* love Aunt Alicia and Aunt Charlotte, but—but I want to live here!'

Mrs Trevennor caught Gerry closely to her. 'And so you shall, my darling!' she said. 'Listen, little girl, to what Uncle Arthur has to say to you.'

The rector smiled at the small, bewildered face. 'I have a letter from your great-aunts, Gerry,' he said. 'Your great-aunt Alicia has seen a very clever doctor, and he says that she must never live in England again. They have decided to buy the house they are renting at present and make their home in Madeira, and as they do not want to interfere with your education, they have decided to agree to a suggestion of mine made a short while ago to them, and to leave you with us until your school-days are over.'

Gerry went from red to white, and then back to red again. 'Oh!' she gasped; 'it seems too good to be true! But sha'n't I be a horrid expense?'

The rector smiled. 'No, dear. When I wrote we wanted to keep you, and treat you as our own; but your great-aunts insist that some return shall be made, so they are going to educate Jill, and now she will be able to go to college and become a doctor, just as she has always wished.'

Just what Gerry would have said to this will never be known, for at that moment the study door burst open, and the entire Rectory family, headed by Jill and Geoff, came pouring in. The rector had told the news to Margaret just a few minutes before, and while he had been telling Gerry she had informed her brothers and sisters what was going to happen.

With a yell of delight Jill grabbed her chum round the neck; while the others, catching hold of their father and mother, and dragging them into it, made a circle and danced round them.

'Three cheers for Gerry!' shouted Paul when at last all had stopped for sheer breathlessness; and they were given, albeit somewhat pantingly.

'Speech! Speech!' cried the rector mischievously.

Instantly his cry was taken up from all parts of the room. Gerry looked round her with glowing cheeks and starry eyes. 'Oh,' she cried, 'I said that yesterday was the gloriousest day ever, but to-day is gloriouser still! I love you all, and I'm ever so glad that I did come to the Rectory!'

THE END